PLEASE ME

DESIRED BY THE BILLIONAIRE (LOVER BOYS ROMANCE)

MICHELLE LOVE

HOT AND STEAMY ROMANCE

CONTENTS

About the Author — vii
Sign Up to Receive Free Books — ix

Blurb — 1
1. Chapter One — 3
2. Chapter Two — 15
3. Chapter Three — 24
4. Chapter Four — 34
5. Chapter Five — 41
6. Chapter Six — 52
7. Chapter Seven — 58
8. Chapter Eight — 64
9. Chapter Nine — 71
10. Chapter Ten — 78
11. Chapter Eleven — 82
12. Chapter Twelve — 90
13. Chapter Thirteen — 96
14. Chapter Fourteen — 102
15. Chapter Fifteen — 109
16. Chapter Sixteen — 116
17. Chapter Seventeen — 125
18. Chapter Eighteen — 135
19. Chapter Nineteen — 140
20. Chapter Twenty — 142
21. Chapter Twenty-One — 148
22. Chapter Twenty-Two — 151
23. Chapter Twenty-Three — 156

Sign Up to Receive Free Books — 159
Preview of Rockstar Untamed — 160
Part one — 162

Other Books By This Author   193
About the Author   195
Copyright   197

Made in "The United States by:

Michelle Love

© Copyright 2020 – Michelle Love

ISBN: 978-1-64808-090-6

ALL RIGHTS RESERVED. No part of this publication may be reproduced or transmitted in any form whatsoever, electronic, or mechanical, including photocopying, recording, or by any informational storage or retrieval system without express written, dated and signed permission from the author

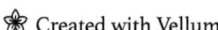 Created with Vellum

ABOUT THE AUTHOR

Mrs. Love writes about smart, sexy women and the hot alpha billionaires who love them. She has found her own happily ever after with her dream husband and adorable 6 and 2 year old kids.
Currently, Michelle is hard at work on the next book in the series, and trying to stay off the Internet.
"Thank you for supporting an indie author. Anything you can do, whether it be writing a review, or even simply telling a fellow reader that you enjoyed this. Thanks

Facebook
facebook.com/HotAndSteamyRomance

SIGN UP TO RECEIVE FREE BOOKS

Sign Up to Receive Free E-Books and Audiobook Codes.

Would you like to read **The Unexpected Nanny, Dirty Little Virgin** and **other romance books** for **free**?

You can sign up to receive these free e-books and audiobooks by typing this link into your browser:

https://www.steamyromance.info/free-books-and-audiobooks-hot-and-steamy/

Or this one:

https://www.steamyromance.info/the-unexpected-nanny-free/

BLURB

He's the most exciting man I've met in a long time—and the most dangerous. His reputation precedes him, and I have a job to do—keep my client out of trouble and out of Stone Vanderberg's newspaper column.
But, God, no one told me he was this magnetic, this sensual, with his machismo such a turn on.
Every time he is near me, my body betrays my own promise not to let him near me.
I crave him...
I don't know how much longer I'll be able to resist him...
... or even if I want to.
I'm supposed to be working but all I think of is what Stone Vanderberg wants to do to me.
And what I am desperate to do with him...

Following a story to Cannes in the south of France, renowned journalist and billionaire playboy, Stone Vanderburg, is enchanted when he meets a beautiful young woman, Nanouk Songbird. The attraction between them is immediate and undeniable, and they have a sensual, thrilling affair.

Stone Vanderberg. That's the name that causes excitement amongst the Hollywood types flocking to the south of France—and with good reason. Am I cocky and arrogant? Sure. But I don't believe in false modesty, and I know I'm a good-looking guy, I know my body is rock-hard, and my cock has legendary status.

I use that name to get what I want—and what I want is *her*... Nanouk Songbird may not be like the flashy actress types that I usually get into my bed—but then again, she's just a human, too. She won't be able to resist me, I know it. Oh yeah, she'll be in my bed before the end of the week, moaning and crying out my name over and over as I f*ck her into submission...

Yeah, she won't be able to resist me...won't she?

CHAPTER ONE

Cannes, France...

STONE VANDERBERG WONDERED, as he did every year, why he came to this film festival. It wasn't as if his long and successful journalistic career had focused on moviemaking, or even celebrity, but he had a fascination with the self-congratulatory ways of the movie stars, directors, and producers who flooded the south of France every May.

One year, almost twelve years ago, he'd written a sarcastic, cynical piece for The New Yorker which had proved wildly popular, and ever since, it became one of the most anticipated stories to come out of the festival every year.

Even the stars and studio bigwigs loved being roasted by Stone Vanderberg—all publicity is *good* publicity, after all—and, for Stone, there were always the perks. He stayed at the *InterContinental Carlton* on the seafront in the Sean Connery suite every year—paid for by the magazine, of course—and there was no shortage of beautiful women eager to bed the handsome writer.

Stone Vanderberg was the eldest son of a Long Island billionaire—the Vanderbergs were old money going generations back who rivalled the Gettys and Rockefellers in terms of prestige and money. Stone and his younger brother Ted, a movie agent, might be heirs to billions, but they stood on their own two feet in the world due to their well-earned international reputations as hard-working, hard-playing lotharios.

Now, Stone sat on his hotel balcony, watching the hordes of tourists and movie people mill around on *La Croisette Boulevard* below him. It was hot already at seven a.m. He'd spend the day watching and listening to the actors and actresses who were out in force to promote their movies. Stone would be invited multiple times to dinner or for drinks, or as he had found out, asked outright to have sex with them—by both the actress *and* the actors.

He had that kind of magnetism. Stone stood six-feet-six, with a broad-shouldered, ripped body from working out at four A.M. every day. At forty, with his dark-brown hair flecked with grey, his dark navy-blue eyes intense, Stone used his machismo, his power, to get what he wanted, and he made no apology for it. He liked hard work and fucking—*especially* fucking. He'd never married because, as he told interviewers, why would he want to settle for just one woman when he could have many? He knew he was arrogant, but he justified it with his charm.

Stone, contrary to his confident demeanor, actually believed in getting more bees with honey, than by jackbooting around. He made sure his conquests were clear that it was just for a night, and he always treated them well in the morning. His colleagues, especially his subordinates, adored him—he was a fair, inclusive employer who paid above the odds and nurtured his staff and their dreams. His personal assistant, Shanae, a gorgeous blonde from Charleston who dressed like someone from Dallas or Dynasty back in the Eighties, all shoulder pads and power suits, was a firecracker who mocked Stone mercilessly and hilariously to his face but was as fiercely loyal as a bulldog. Shanae and Stone shared a sibling-like relationship—despite Stone's man-whoring ways, Shanae had made it clear when she took the job that sex wasn't on the cards.

"I don't shit where I eat," she had said to him during the interview. "I know about men like you, Stone Vanderberg, and that monster in your pants is never going to get near my good girl."

Stone had given her the job on the spot. Now, checking the time back in New York, he debated calling her, knowing she would still be awake, playing retro videos games and eating peanut butter cookies.

Maybe not. She wouldn't thank him for the interruption. Instead, he went back into his room and into the bedroom of the suite. Last night's conquest was just waking up. He smiled at her.

"Hey, Holly."

Holly was a fun redhead who grinned back at him. "Hey, dude. Listen, I'll get out of your hair in a sec, but I need to shower. I have a meeting at ten, and my hotel is way out of town."

"Sure thing, honey. Come join me?"

Holly laughed. "If I do that, we'll end up fucking and I'll be late. Can I just hop in quick?"

"Of course."

She kissed him as she passed him and reached down to squeeze his cock. "Great night, babe."

"Right back at you."

Stone heard the shower running and sighed, content. This was what he liked—great sex followed by a friendly chat in the morning and no expectations. Holly had been an exceptional fuck, too—athletic, uninhibited, and good-humored. Gorgeous, too: punky, tattooed, different from his usual choice.

He thought about that now. *What is my 'usual' choice?* He smirked to himself. Beautiful. Sexy. With any luck, *not* skin and bones. With all the actresses being coerced into sample sizes by designers for this shindig, finding Holly who wasn't a size zero had been a miracle. But, Stone considered, that was probably why she wasn't doing as well in her career as some of the skeletons in designer duds haunting the festival.

"Hey, Hols? When you get back to the States, call me. We'll set up a profile piece for you. Get your name out there."

Holly stuck her head out of the bathroom door. "Is this a *thank you for sex* thing?"

Stone grinned. "No, it's a *good things should happen to a great woman like you* thing."

Holly flushed with pleasure. "Don't worry, I won't tell the world the great Stone Vanderberg is a teddy bear." She kissed him. "Thanks for an amazing fuck, Stone. You're the best."

"Oh, I know."

Holly rolled her eyes, laughing. "Later, babe."

THE ROOM RANG with silence after she'd gone. Stone considered that he wouldn't mind running into Holly again one day—she was a breath of fresh air. He grabbed his notepad—he was an old-school kind of writer—and headed out to wander through the crowds. Snagging his accreditation from the appropriate festival tent, he headed to the International Village, a series of pavilions where movie people networked and promoted their films.

In the Italian tent, he saw Cosimo DeLuca chatting to a group of producers. Stone waited until the other man was free before greeting his old friend. "Cos, you look ten years younger."

Cosimo grinned. "That would be Biba."

"How is she?"

"Pregnant again. Planned, I should add. We can't wait. Now that this latest movie is in the can, and after this thing, I can go home to Italy and forget about the movies for a few months." He looked around. "I've been trying to grab Eliso—I'd like him to consider a role, but I keep missing him."

Eliso Patini was perhaps Italy's most famous actor, but he was notoriously private. He was also Stone's best friend. Stone shrugged. "You know if you call him, he'll always call *you* back, Cos. I think you're on the list of five people he *will* return a call for."

They both laughed. "You doing your yearly article?"

Stone nodded. "It's been disappointingly drama free this year."

"I might have a tip. Apart from the fact that Stella is here and looking to upstage Jennifer Lawrence... *again*," Cosimo laughed, "I hear Sheila Maffey is here and very unhappy."

"About representation?"

"Yup. She has a point. Not one of the judges this year is either a woman or a minority. It's all looking very white." Cosimo shook his head. "In this day and age, it's a disgrace."

"No arguments here, although two middle-aged white men probably shouldn't be the champions for it," Stone said with a sigh.

"We can be allies. Anyway, the studio sent along a lawyer with Sheila for her press interviews. The poor kid. She looks like she would blow away in a breeze, but she seems to be fending off the worst and keeping Sheila in line."

"They sent a woman to silence a woman?"

"No, actually, the lawyer seems to be completely on Sheila's side, so that's good. Kid just clarifies language. You know Sheila though, it won't be too long before she blows up."

Stone nodded his head, thinking. "Thanks for the tip, man. Might be worth a look."

"Listen, let's do dinner before the end of this thing. I have to get to my next suck-up meeting." Cosimo slapped Stone's shoulder. "I'm just so relieved I'm not in competition this year. Later, my brother."

"Later, buddy."

As Cosimo walked away, he turned back and called out. "The Maffey thing is at *La Salon des Independents*, down on *Rue Louis Perrissol*. Sheila's on a roll. You should still catch them there."

"Thanks, man."

STONE WALKED the few blocks to the café. Years of pounding Cannes' side streets had made him an expert at the layout, and he had been to that bar before. The maître d' greeted him and asked him if he wanted a table.

"Miss Maffey's here?" Stone's voice was even, but he slipped a fifty-euro note to the woman. She smiled.

"Yes, sir. I believe there is a table nearby."

"Good girl." He winked at her, turning on his patented charm and she simpered at him. She led him to a table across from Sheila, who, as Cosimo predicted, was making her case to an unfortunate journalist.

Stone sat down and glanced over casually. At first, he just registered Sheila, magnificent in white, her dark hair piled up on her head, her elegance complimented by discreet but priceless jewels. From Stone's practiced eye, he estimated Sheila was wearing at least two million dollars-worth of gems. He hid a smile. Sheila was class and elegance but for a *breakfast* meeting? She was savvy; she knew how to make an impression, Stone had to give her that.

Then his attention was caught by the young woman sitting

next to her, and his stomach felt like someone had driven a sledgehammer into it.

She was caramel-skinned, and her long dark hair was pulled into a messy bun at the nape of her neck. Huge, dark, soulful eyes, a rose-pink mouth, the last vestiges of puppy face making her face look younger than he supposed she was, but Stone felt as if his breath was hitching and failing. She was achingly beautiful but not in an obvious way like the actresses he knew—indeed, her face was make-up free—but in a soft, natural way. She was also the saddest person he had ever seen.

Stone caught himself staring, and when she looked up and met his gaze, a frisson crackled in the air between them. He watched as her cheeks blushed a rosy color, and she looked away. *Gotcha,* he thought, then felt bad. She wasn't someone to catch in a trap.

The young woman glanced back at him, and he saw recognition dawn in her eyes. She glanced at Sheila who was in mid-rant, and then suddenly stood. "This interview is ending. Right now."

Both Sheila and the interviewer look startled, but Stone grinned, unrepentant. His girl had recognized who he was and what he was doing, and she was doing her job, protecting her client. He watched her speak quietly to Sheila, who glanced over at him and rolled her eyes. Stone gave her a wave, and Sheila laughed, shaking her head.

"Well, Goddamn, Stone Vanderberg. I might have known."

To Stone's chagrin, her companion was making her way out of the bar with the journalist, and as Sheila was clearly set on talking to him, he had missed his shot at finding out who the beautiful stranger was. Sheila, her glossy black skin clear and glowing, sized him up. They'd had a thing years ago, but Sheila was even more of a commitment-phobe than he was.

Stone kissed her cheek. "Sheila, always good to see you."

"Wish I could say the same. You going to eviscerate me in your piece? I mean, I don't mind, but what I'm ranting about this time actually means something."

"Nope, just wanted to say hi. Cosimo told me you were here. And for what it's worth, I'm with you on representation."

Her expression softened. "Good."

Stone nodded after her companion. "Studio sending you a muzzle?"

Sheila looked surprised. "Nan? Nope, quite the opposite. She's an entertainment lawyer, but she wants to move into human rights. She figures supporting me with this campaign gets her on the map. Kid's young, but she's tenacious."

"Nan?"

Sheila smiled. "Nanouk, and you leave her alone, Vanderberg. She's way too good for you, you slut."

Stone laughed, not offended in the least. "They always are, Sheila. Come on, I'll buy you lunch."

Nanouk Songbird dumped her laptop on the desk in her tiny hotel room and flopped onto the bed. She hated being in Cannes and dealing with so many people around. Living in New York, she told herself that she should be used to crowds, but here, with so many people packed into the small coastal city all wanting to see the same thing, she felt claustrophobic.

And then there was the added irritant of Stone Vanderberg. She knew all about him, of course: the billionaire journalist from the powerful Vanderberg family. They were New York, and more specifically, Oyster Bay, Long Island. She'd grown up across town from their compound, in a tiny wood-frame house with her sister, Etta, who raised Nan after their parents were killed in a car wreck when Etta was eighteen and Nan was twelve. Etta raised the bewildered Nan all by herself, and Nan adored her older sister, and they were happy.

Then, one night, Etta was raped as she walked home from her job at the local library. She was unable to bear the trauma, and a few weeks later, when then-eighteen-year-old Nan came home from school, she found her sister dead from an overdose of sleeping tablets. She left a note.

I'm so sorry, baby bird, but I can't go on. Fly free with all my love, little one.

Nan was left alone and numb. On autopilot, she went through the motions of graduating from high school with a 4.0 GPA and applying to colleges. She got into Harvard Law on a scholarship. There, she met her best friend, Raoul—an easy-going Jewish boy from old money who adored her on sight. Raoul was openly gay, and Nan felt safe with him. The trauma of Etta's rape stayed with her, and although she made friends, she avoided dating, to the chagrin of the college boys who were drawn to her honey-skinned beauty. Nan's heritage—a father from Punjab, India, and a Shinnecock Indian mother—made her beauty exotic and alluring, but she consistently played down her looks, not wanting to be judged by them.

It was a habit she kept up even now. She got up and stripped out of her elegant work suit, hanging it up carefully. She was a jeans and T-shirt girl, and only now could she feel herself relaxing as she undid her hair from its bun and let it fall around her. Thick and lustrous, she knew she should get it cut into a more professional style—it was always messy—but it was her security blanket.

She made herself some herbal tea and pushed open the small door to the tiny balcony outside. The hotel was further into town but if she craned her neck around the side of the building, she could just make out the ocean. No matter. She sat in one of the chairs and sipped her tea. It was quieter here than on the seafront, and she reveled in the peace.

Now, away from Sheila, Nan could think about Stone Vanderberg. She hadn't expected him to be quite so... magnetic. *Yup, that's the word.* He was tall, at least a foot taller than her, and his broad, obviously worked-out body was the stuff of magazine covers—even the way his casual sweater and jeans hung on his body was like an Abercrombie and Fitch commercial.

His dark blue eyes had met hers, and Nan had felt a thrill go through her. A pulse had begun to beat between her legs, astonishing her. Was this what they called the lightning bolt moment? Or, more likely, she grinned to herself, it was just a primal lust instinct. She wondered what it would be like to be fucked by him. She could imagine he always insisted on being dominant—and to be honest, she wouldn't mind that. His machismo, the slight air of danger in him...

Stop. She was getting turned on, and Stone Vanderberg was way, *way* out her league.

There was a knock at her door. Sighing, Nan got up. Her heart sank when she opened the door. Duggan Smollett, the studio's representative in Cannes this year, smiled at her. Nan's skin prickled. Since her arrival, he had hit on her virtually every time they had met, and he gave her the creeps. His small, silver eyes darted around, and his face was bloated from drink and coke. By the looks of it, he was high now—the sniffling and nose wiping a dead giveaway.

"Hey. Nannynook."

Ugh. "Hello, Duggan, how can I help you?" She deliberately kept her voice even—and her body rigid, preventing him from coming in. He smiled at her.

"Gonna let me in?"

"I'm taking some private time, Duggan." She didn't care if she had to be rude; he wasn't getting in. She didn't work for him.

"Oh, okay. Well, look, I was just checking in. How did the interview with Sheila and *Time Out* go?"

"Fine, nothing to report. I sent you the e-mail a little while ago." *Which you saw and then decided to come to my room to intimidate me. Asshole.*

Duggan smiled nastily. "Didn't see it. Well, okay. The premier's tonight, and I was wondering if you'd like to have dinner with me afterward."

Not a chance in hell. "I'm sorry, Duggan, Sheila's invited me to dine with her."

"Maybe some other night."

Nan didn't answer him. "Is there anything else?"

"No, no, just checking in. Well... bye for now."

"Goodbye, Duggan." There was a little satisfaction in closing the door in his face, but she double-locked it to be sure. Duggan was a predator and a coked-up one at that. Not worth the risk.

Nan found Sheila had sent her a message.

Warning, Sneaky Smollett is looking for you. Sorry, kiddo. Still on for tonight? S x

Nan smiled. Sheila was the best part of her job at the moment. She loved the actress' passion for her art, for her causes. Sheila wasn't a woman who sat down and shut up. She spoke out no matter who tried to put her down.

She was also one of the kindest people Nan had ever met, and they had bonded almost immediately upon acquaintance. Nan had to admit to herself that Sheila reminded her of Etta so much that she had almost morphed the two women in her mind. *Don't get too attached,* she told herself, *Sheila might be a friend, but this is still a job.*

Nan checked her watch. She had a few hours before the premiere. Jet lag was catching up with her, and she eagerly crawled under the comforter and curled up to grab a couple of hours sleep.

. . .

THE DREAM BEGAN PLEASANTLY ENOUGH. She was walking a red carpet alone with the cool breeze blowing off the ocean. No one else was around, and the peace was incredible. Then she saw him—Stone Vanderberg. He held his hand out to her, and she took it. He drew her into his arms and kissed her, his mouth sweet, his lips passionate against hers.

Then smiling, he turned her around and locked his arms around her. Nan saw Duggan walking towards her, smirking nastily. She began to panic, but Stone put his lips to her ear. "It's alright, darling. It'll only hurt for a moment..."

She began to scream as Duggan drove a knife deep into her over and over...

Nan awoke, shaking and terrified.

CHAPTER TWO

Eliso Patini, movie star, grinned up at his girlfriend as she lay on top of him, breathless and sweating from fucking. He bunched a thick swath of her honey-gold hair around his fist. "God, I love you, Beulah Tegan."

Beulah smiled. "Glad to hear it. Now, come on, old man! Let's go again."

Eliso laughed. As Beulah stroked his cock back into full erection, he ran his hands gently down her curvaceous body. They had been together a little over a year, and in that time, Eliso had found himself a changed man. Yeah, it was a cliché: a movie star with a *Sports Illustrated* model, but Beulah Tegan—a cockney from London—was so much more than a beautiful face and a stop-the-traffic body. She was funny, erudite, and above all, kind, and Eliso had fallen for her as soon as they had met.

Eliso himself was a one of a kind, an actor who didn't sleep around, who didn't cheat when he was in a relationship, despite the fact he regularly ranked in the top ten 'Most Gorgeous Men in the World' lists. His easy-going manner belied a towering acting talent which could make an audience laugh one moment, then leave them weeping inconsolably the next.

His shaggy dark curls and large expressive green eyes were magnets to women, as well as his storied prowess in bed, but Eliso had always longed for a partner rather than just a quick lay. As fate would have it, when the year before he'd been seated next to Beulah at a fashion show and found her to be as bored as he was by the fashion and the vapid people, he knew he'd found a kindred spirit.

Beulah straddled him now and impaled herself onto his cock with a shuddering moan. "God, you're huge," she said, "I swear your cock gets bigger every day. Fuck, that's good."

She was riding him, taking him deeper. He stroked her flat belly, cupped her full breasts, and gazed up at her. Her tawny hair tumbled around her, and Eliso wondered if he'd ever seen such a beautiful sight. Beulah grinned down at him. "You have mushy in your eyes."

"Wanna get married?"

Beulah laughed. "How come you always ask me that when we're fucking?"

"Because I mean it. Marry me."

Beulah shook her head. "Not yet, sexy boy. We both have too much to do in our careers yet."

"Screw my career."

"I'd rather screw your monster cock. Besides, I couldn't take you away from your adoring fans—and, seriously, Eli, you're right on the cusp of something huge. Unlike me," she giggled then, "I'm *actually* on something huge."

She began to move faster, tightening her cunt around his cock, and Eliso groaned as she began to milk him, his cock pumping thick creamy cum deep into her belly. Beulah gave a long groan of ecstasy as she came. As both tried to catch their breath, Beulah detached herself and lay down next to him, stroking his face. "I love you, Eli, so, *so* much. But before we do the whole domesticated thing, we need to finish what we started. Then we can build a family with no regrets."

"Smart girl."

"You know it."

Eliso glanced at the clock. "What time did we say we're meeting Stone?"

"At the premiere. Don't make that face, we have to go to the premiere—you promised your agent. If you're a good boy and pose nicely, I'll blow you in the restrooms."

Eliso broke out laughing—that comment was just like Beulah. She had no time for airs and graces. "Deal."

FLASHBULBS IN THEIR FACES, Eliso and Beulah did their job, smiling for the cameras and even kissing when they were asked. During the entire time, they kept up a softly spoken private conversation, mocking the paparazzi, and talking dirty to each other.

Finally, inside the *Palais des Festivals et des Congrès,* Beulah made good on her promise, sucking his cock in one of the stalls of the restrooms, both of them giggling and laughing, then Eliso fucked her against the cool tile, kissing her passionately.

Eventually they made their way to the auditorium. Eliso saw Stone and made his way over to him with Beulah on his arm. The two men hugged. "Hey dude." Stone grinned at his friend, and Eliso introduced him to Beulah, who sized him up.

"Yep, you'll do," she said in her cockney accent and Stone laughed.

"Glad I come up to scratch. Listen, how come I've only just been introduced?"

Eliso looked sheepish. "Sorry, man, I know it's been too long. Time got away from me."

Stone grinned. "Come on, let's watch this thing, then we can start drinking."

"Yeah," Beulah said to Eliso, "I like this one."

They laughed and went to find their seats.

Stone sat down next to his friends and chatted with them until the lights went down. The director had just walked out onto the stage to introduce the movie when a commotion was heard at the door, and Sheila Maffey walked in, smiling, calling her apologies to the director who took the interruption in good grace.

Sheila waved and found her seat, and behind her, Stone saw a very red-faced Nan, trying to disappear into the floor. She looked up before she sat and met his gaze. Her color deepened, and she quickly sat down, out of his eye-line. Stone smiled to himself. He knew Sheila would be at the party after the movie and hoped her lovely companion would join her there. He would make sure to introduce himself properly this time.

That was easier said than done. Nan was clever enough to stay out of all limelight at the party. Frustrated, Stone searched the crowd for her, but couldn't see her anywhere. Beulah excused herself to use the restroom, and Stone looked on as Eliso gazed after her. He grinned at his friend. "You are in love."

Eliso nodded. "I don't deny it, man. I'm done, she's the one." He laughed, then studied his friend. "What about you?"

Stone shrugged. "There's a very beginning of something... I think. I don't know. I've never spoken one word to the girl I'm interested in."

Eliso's eyebrows shot up. "What's this? Stone Vanderberg has a crush?"

Stone snorted. "I wouldn't call it that—just an interest."

"Is she here?"

"Somewhere. She's with Sheila, a lawyer from the studio."

Eliso nodded. "Oh, the girl who looked like she was about to die from embarrassment?"

"That's the one."

Eliso nodded approvingly. "She's beautiful. Go for it, man. About time you found your Beulah."

Stone chuckled. "Yeah, I don't think it'll be quite that magical, but I like your optimism."

"It happens, man. 'The one.' It's a real thing."

"If you say so."

HE FINALLY SPOTTED her just before midnight. Her long hair was down, and she'd kicked off her heels and was sitting outside on the balcony, hidden away behind a palm. Her eyes were closed, and she was leaning back against the cool stone. The night was much cooler now with a breeze picking up from the ocean. Stone tried not to notice how her nipples were hard and showing against her dark burgundy dress.

"Hi."

Her eyes flew open, and there was that beautiful blush again. "Hi."

Stone held his hand out. "Stone Vanderberg."

A slight smile. "I know who you are, Mr. Vanderberg." She stood up and shook his hand. God, she was tiny. "Nanouk Songbird."

"Hi, Nanouk. Beautiful name."

She nodded—she's obviously heard that before, and he cursed himself silently for his unoriginality. "I guess you knew who I was when you shut down Sheila's interview. Let me put your mind at rest. Off the record. All of it."

"Thank you, I appreciate that. Although, I'm sure if you were to write something supporting Sheila's campaign, she wouldn't mind."

Stone smiled. "And the studio?"

Nan didn't answer, only smirked, and Stone decided he liked this woman very much. She had a rebellious streak. "Are you enjoying the party?"

"To be honest, I've never enjoyed this part. Too many people."

"Where are you from?"

She laughed, and it lit up her face. "New York."

Stone looked bemused. "Too many people… here?"

"I know, I know, the irony. But at least in New York, they ignore you. Here, everyone is after something." She shuddered and for a moment, Stone saw the sadness return to her eyes. Nan cleared her throat and shook her head to dismiss whatever she was feeling. She studied him. "Actually, we have something in common."

"We do?"

"Oyster Bay."

Stone was entirely taken by surprise, and for some reason, he was delighted. "You're from there?"

Nan nodded. "I still live there."

Stone smiled. "I don't get back as much as I would like to. Maybe I should," he said, idly and waited for her reaction.

"Nan?"

Damn. Damn. Damn. Stone looked around to see Sheila bearing down on them. Was it his imagination or did Nan look a little annoyed at the interruption, too? In a flash, her expression was smoothed out into a friendly smile. "Hey, Sheila. Did you need something?"

"No, darling, I just wanted to say goodnight." Sheila eyed Stone. "Didn't I warn you away, Vanderberg?" She laughed aloud and kissed Nan's cheek. "Still, the night is young. Enjoy, both of you." She winked at Stone as she disappeared back into the party.

Nan's phone bleeped, and she sighed, checking it. "God, what now?" She mumbled and groaned. "Damn it." She looked at Stone, and he saw a little regret in her eyes. "Mr. Vanderberg, I'm sorry, you'll have to excuse me. It's still mid-afternoon in Los Angeles, and my boss wants to talk to me. It was nice to meet you."

"And you. And it's Stone, for the future."

She shook his hand, and he held onto her hand a beat too long. "...and you can call me Nan. Goodbye... Stone."

"Bye, Nan."

Her perfume, jasmine, wafted over him as she grabbed her shoes and passed him. He wanted to grab her hand, pull her into his arms, and kiss that beautiful mouth. Yup. He was enchanted. Nan Songbird was someone he wanted to get to know better, and he knew he wouldn't be satisfied until she was naked in his arms, in his bed, and crying out his name as he fucked her into paradise.

NAN WASN'T PAYING attention as she walked along the corridor to her hotel room. She was checking her text messages but hadn't read a single one properly. She was thinking of Stone Vanderberg's hand in hers, the feel of his skin on hers. The way he looked at her made her think dirty, dirty thoughts, and it taken all of her self-control not to press her body up to his masculine frame. God, the man was gorgeous.

She fumbled the key card, and as she bent to pick it up, she felt arms ago around her waist. "Yeah, baby, that's more like it."

Duggan. She struggled against his arms, but he held her

close, grabbing the key card and opening the door. He threw her in before slamming it closed behind him.

Survival instinct kicked in, and Nan scrambled across the room. Duggan was twice her size. "Get out!" she said firmly, but of course, he ignored her and came for her, hands clamping down onto her arms and dragging her toward the bedroom. As he yanked roughly at her dress, Nan felt the fabric rip. *No. This was not going to happen.*

With all her strength, she jammed her thumbs into Duggan's eyes, clamping her fingers around his head, digging her nails in as hard as she could. Duggan gave a roar of pain and tried to shake her hands off, but Nan, her face grim, locked them harder around him.

"Unless you want me to blind you, motherfucker, you will let me go! Right. Now."

Duggan's hands dropped. Pushing hard, Nan walked him backwards towards her door, not letting go. "Open the door, Duggan."

"I can't fucking see, bitch."

"Feel your way," she snarled, "You seem to be very handsy. *Feel* for the door handle, asshole."

Duggan got the door open, and Nan forced him into the hallway. As she released his head, he managed to punch her hard in the stomach. As she doubled over with a grunt and he lunged for her again, she heard shouting, and two huge jocks came bearing down and dragged Duggan away down the hall. A woman, apparently with the jocks, came to help her up. "Are you okay?" American.

Nan shook her head. "This asshole just tried to rape me."

Duggan was struggling, but even in his coked-up condition, he was no match for his captors. The other woman took Nan into her room and called down for the manager of the hotel.

After Duggan was taken away, and the hotel manager

finished apologizing profusely, Nan called her boss in Los Angeles and told him what had happened. He was appalled. "Nan, I cannot tell you how sorry I am." There was a pause. "Do you want to press charges?"

Nan sighed. She knew full well what Clive was asking. The studio would rather not have a scandal on its hands when its films were in competition. "No. But I want assurances Duggan will be dealt with, and I want to change hotels. I don't feel safe here."

Relieved, Clive told her he'd call her back, and within an hour, she was being moved to the Carlton and into the Grace Kelly suite. Nan was a little overwhelmed, but the hotel manager assured her all was well. "Miss Bellucci checked out of the suite this morning, Miss Songbird."

Nan wondered how much the studio had to lay down to get her this room and which A-lister got bumped. But she didn't care. Yes, they paid for her silence, but she was safe and far away from Duggan. Clive told her the man had been fired. "We take sexual assault very seriously, Nan. Anything else you need—just say the word."

Nan was happy just to be out of Duggan's reach. The Carlton had security out the wazoo because of the fleet of A-listers staying there. Her suite was incredible—more luxurious than Nan had ever experienced, but all she cared about was the freedom. She stepped out onto the balcony; at this hotel, the view was panoramic. She looked at her watch; it was almost four A.M. now, and she had to be up by seven to meet Sheila.

Nan felt utterly wrecked by exhaustion. She quickly showered, got her clothes ready for the morning, set an alarm, and then fell into bed and an uneasy sleep.

3

CHAPTER THREE

Stone couldn't get Nan Songbird out of his head. Damn Sheila for interrupting, and damn that phone call from her boss. They had been connecting, for Chrissakes, and without the interruptions, he would be waking up in this bed with a beautiful woman, instead of alone.

He told himself Nan was no different from the rest of the women he bedded. He couldn't get involved—not now.

But Nan was haunting him. Stone was determined he would have her before he left Cannes... it was just... he didn't know if he could forget her once he left. *Damn it, she's just another girl,* he told himself. He got out of bed and went to work out, pounding the treadmill hard, trying to get the excess tension out of him. His piece was coming together; he knew he could finish up today, then kickback for the last few days of the festival.

He met Eliso and Beulah for lunch downstairs in the Grand Salon and learned they were leaving the next day. "Eli's been at me to visit Italy with him...meet the parents. Scary." Beulah didn't look at all scared, and Eliso grinned at her.

"They're going to love you."

Stone smiled at the pair of lovebirds, but for a strange

moment, he felt lonely. He had avoided all attachments for so long that seeing his brother-in-arms, his wingman Eliso, so in love and deliriously happy, was a stark reminder than he, Stone, didn't have that. Had *never* had that.

He looked up as a movement caught his eye and saw Nan Songbird walk into the restaurant and look around with nervous uncertainty. Stone saw her hesitate, obviously trying to decide whether to stay or cut and run.

"Excuse me a moment." He got up and went over to her. He was gratified by the relief he saw in her eyes that she knew someone. "Hey, Nan, are you okay?"

She smiled at him. God, she was lovely. "I am, thank you. I've just... I've never been in this restaurant before."

"Well, would you like to join us?" He nodded back at the table where Eliso and Beulah were sitting. Beulah grinned at Nan, and Eliso put his hand up in greeting. Nan colored but smiled back at them.

"You're very kind, but no, I'm actually meeting a friend... and there he is. Late as usual." Nan smiled at Stone apologetically. "Thank you, though. It was good to see you again."

Stone touched her cheek with a fingertip. "You, too."

Nan smiled and colored slightly, before stepping away from him somewhat awkwardly.

He watched her walk over to a friendly looking man in a grey suit and hug him. Stone registered that a part of him felt a pang of jealousy even though he had no right, but he soon realized that, judging by the body language between Nan and her lunch companion, there was nothing to be envious of.

Stone went back to his table and to the questions from his friends. "That's your crush?" Beulah said, obviously enjoying Stone's discomfort. "She's gorgeous, mate, and she likes you, I can tell."

"You can tell from twenty feet away?" Eliso sneered at his girlfriend.

Beulah stuck her tongue out at him. "A *woman* can tell." She studied Stone, who was smiling to himself. "You like her."

"I don't know her, but, yeah," he admitted to Eliso's shocked expression and Beulah's victorious cackle, "She intrigues me."

"Yeah, I bet you'll end up 'intriguing' her, too—all day and night."

Stone grinned. "I adore you," he said to Beulah, "Run away with me."

"Just let me get rid of this old man."

Eliso shrugged good-naturedly. "I'll just say that Stone is older than me by fifteen days and leave it at that."

Beulah sighed dramatically. "Guess it'll have to come down to cock size then. Whip 'em out, boys."

Stone and Eliso both pretended to unzip, making Beulah break into raucous laughter. Nearby diners looked around in irritation, but when they saw the gorgeous woman laughing, they soon forgave the noisy table.

NAN SAT down with Raoul in the sunshine, grinning at him. "God, I missed you, Owl. All these damn actors and actresses... I need someone boring and dull like you."

"Oh, ha ha, you little bitch," Raoul grinned at his friend, knowing she was teasing him. "What's up with you? You've aged fifty years! Look at those crow's feet. And your bolt-ons have sagged bad, girl," he nodded at her perfectly perky and entirely natural breasts.

Nan giggled. She adored this man. She had met Raoul when they were in law school, and they quickly become inseparable. Raoul was her best friend, her confidante, her brother. He came from a long line of wealthy New York lawyers, and growing up, he hadn't even questioned his career path. In court, he was a ruthless defense lawyer, grilling witnesses until he broke them. Out of court, however, he was funny and kind. Always searching for Mr. Right, he despaired over Nan's 'tragic' love life. "If only I was straight, Nook."

"If only."

Now, though, he was grilling her about Stone. "So, you like him?"

Nan rolled her eyes. "Dude, I've spoken about six words to the man."

"Nook, don't lie to me. You have *horny* in your eyes. I haven't seen that look since we did that Keanu Reeves marathon at the Majestic back in college."

"That doesn't count," Nan said, deflecting his question. "There isn't a human alive that could resist Keanu."

"True story, but back to Wonderdong Vanderberg. I have heard he is *packing*, girl, so when in Cannes..."

"You are such a pimp. You ever thought about going into the sex trade?"

Raoul grinned. "If it meant you getting laid..." His smile disappeared. "Nook?"

Nan was pale, and she started to tremble. Raoul looked in the direction she was staring. A man was gazing at her, and his expression was anything but friendly. As they watched, he narrowed his eyes at her before turning on his heel and walking off.

"Who the hell was that?"

Nan smiled a brittle grimace. "Duggan Smollett. He's from the studio." She looked down at her hands. "He tried to rape me last night."

"What the fuck?" Instantly, Raoul was furious and halfway out of his chair before Nan dragged him back down.

"I dealt with it, Owl. Sit down. People are staring."

Raoul didn't look happy. "So that explains the Grace Kelly suite. The studio?"

"Yep. Look, it's okay with me. Dealing with the police will just create more of a nuisance, and I can do without that."

Raoul sighed. "God, Nan..."

"I know. Let's change the subject, huh? How's your dad?"

"He's good. In fact, I'm here as a double agent."

Nan grinned at him. "And here I was thinking you were just here to stalk Chris Hemsworth."

"Oh, well, that too, *obviously*," Raoul laughed. He leaned forward, eyes shining. "But even better... Sarah Lund is retiring from Dad's firm in the next six months. He has an opening for a junior partner."

"And Sarah Lund is a..."

"Criminal lawyer. Defense. Interested?"

Nan was elated. "Are you kidding? Of course! Jeez, Raoul... is your dad sure? I mean, I have very little experience in criminal law, but hell, that's what I've wanted to do since I graduated."

"I know, and so does he. He'll have you work side-by-side with him at first to get the experience you need, or as he says, mostly for your own confidence. He believes in you, Nook. We both do."

Nan felt close to tears. Alan Elizondo was one of New York's most successful and well-regarded defense attorneys. He ran a tight ship with a close cohort of hand-picked attorneys and very few chances for young lawyers to break in. That he wanted *her*...

"God, Raoul, I don't know what to say."

Raoul grinned. "Yeah, you do. Say yes. This is what you've wanted. Out of the entertainment business and into criminal law. Congrats, Nook, you deserve it."

NAN WAS STILL on a high later as she met up with Sheila and

went through her schedule for the next few days. Sheila noticed the younger woman's good mood and asked her about it. Nan explained about the job.

"Well, I'll miss you, but I know this is what you wanted, Nan. I'm very happy for you." She hugged Nan. "Just promise we'll stay friends."

"Always," Nan told her with a smile. She stayed for tea with Sheila, and when Sheila went to her next appointment, Nan returned to the Carlton and headed to the elevator. A couple of hours sleep, then maybe a light supper and walk along the waterfront? If she milled in with the crowds, she would feel safer. It was her night off, and she was determined that the thought of Duggan Smollett wouldn't ruin it.

She had just pressed the button for her floor when the elevator door opened again and Stone Vanderberg stepped in. Her heart began to thump hard against her chest. "Hey."

"Hello again. We keep running into each other." God, even his voice made her sex pulse with desire.

"We do. Thank you for your invitation earlier—it was very kind."

"My pleasure." His eyes were intense fixed on hers. "Did you have a good lunch?"

"Very, thanks."

The tension was unbearable. Nan's breath began to quicken. They gazed at each other, and then Stone stepped closer to her and bent his head down toward hers. His mouth was only an inch from hers when the elevator doors opened again and a raft of people, chatting and talking, poured in. The press of the crowd herded Nan and Stone against the back wall of the elevator. With his body pressed against hers and his navy-blue eyes locked on her, Nan couldn't look away. He could have done anything to her, but what he did do made her heart skip a beat.

He took her hand. Linking his fingers in hers, he didn't try to do anything else. He didn't press his groin against hers and any of countless things many other men would have tried—and *had* tried with Nan in an enclosed space. Stone Vanderberg took her hand and *held* it and Nan was lost.

It seemed impossible that, when the elevator stopped on the seventh floor, they wouldn't end up in the same suite. The elevator emptied out and, still holding her hand, Stone led her down the hallway. Nan walked as if in a dream, a dream broken only seconds later by a voice calling her name.

No. No, go away... "Miss Songbird? Miss Songbird? I have an urgent message for you from Miss Maffey."

Nan and Stone stopped, and Nan could have screamed. Stone didn't look happy either as the bellhop handed her a message and left. Nan read the note and sighed. She looked up at Stone. "Sheila got nabbed for an impromptu interview by Jay McInerney. She wants me there. I'm so sorry."

Stone smiled down at her... *God, his smile...* and he cupped her cheek in his hand. "No problem. Dinner, later?"

Nan nodded. "How about I meet you at this restaurant?" She showed him the note.

"The *Rue du Suquet*? Perfect." He stroked her cheek, seeming to hesitate. "I want to kiss you so badly, Nan Songbird, but I think if I do, I won't be able to stop myself from... and I don't want to get you fired."

Nan laughed softly. "Anticipation, Stone Vanderberg."

"Anticipation. Ten P.M?"

"Until then."

She was still smiling, and her body seemed to burn with excitement as she took a cab to the *Rue du Suquet*. She walked into the restaurant and asked for Sheila. The maître d' looked confused. "Is Ms. Maffey here? Please wait a moment, Mademoiselle."

He returned a moment later. "I'm sorry, Mademoiselle. Ms. Maffey isn't here."

Nan frowned and pulled the note from her purse, checking it again. She looked apologetically at the man. "I'm sorry, maybe the booking is under Mr. McInerney? Jay McInerney?"

The man looked embarrassed. "No, I'm sorry."

Nan nodded, her face burning. *What the hell?* "No matter. I'm sorry to bother you. Listen... while I'm here, do you have a reservation for ten P.M. available?"

The maître d' looked uncertain, and Nan, feeling guilty, decided to use the only tool at her disposal. "It's for Mr. Vanderberg. Stone Vanderberg."

The maître d's expression cleared, and he smiled. "Of course, an old friend. Table for?"

"Two, please. A private booth if one is available." If she was going to name drop, she was going to go all the way.

"Of course." The maître d' was looking at her with more respect now, and Nan smothered a laugh. Oh, the life of a billionaire. She didn't think Stone would mind.

Nan checked her watch. It was almost nine P.M. Mentally cursing herself for not taking Stone's cell phone number, she went across the street to another bar and called Sheila. Voicemail. She shook her head. *What the hell was going on?*

Nan sighed. Well, she had time for a drink and to relax before her date with Stone. She ordered a martini and sat down.

STONE WAS STILL SMILING to himself as he went down to the bar in the Carlton. As he sat at the bar, he recognized Nan's lunch date already seated there and introduced himself. Raoul Elizondo smiled at him.

"Good to meet you, Mr. Vanderberg."

"Stone, please, and likewise. We have a friend in common."

Raoul nodded, his merry eyes dancing. "Ah."

Stone grinned. "Is it that obvious?"

"That you like our Nanouk? Yes, but I think it may be mutual."

"Sorry if I seem presumptuous."

"You don't, and I'm all for it. Nan and myself have been friends since college, and this is the first time I've noticed that particular gleam in her eye. Sorry," Raoul laughed when Stone's eyebrows shot up, "I'm not one for beating around the bush, so to speak. You like her, she likes you—a done deal. Just don't hurt her, blah, blah."

Stone decided he liked this man very much. "Nan has good taste in friends."

Raoul raised his glass. "Thank you." His smile faltered a little. "I'm just thankful that, well, someone will look out for her. I have to leave in the morning, and with that Smollett guy still hanging around..."

Stone's heart gave a lurch. "Who?"

Raoul hesitated. "She'll probably kill me for telling you this..." He told Stone about Smollett's attempted rape of Nan. "He was fired by the studio, and I'm worried he'll take it out on her."

Jesus. "She didn't mention it, but then, really, we just met. But I'll look out for her, don't worry."

"Sorry to dump."

"Seriously, man, I'm glad you told me. I..." Stone trailed off as he saw Sheila Maffey walk into the bar. For a second, he waited for Nan to follow her, and as Sheila saw him and walked over, his heart began to beat a little faster. Unease crept over him. "Hey, Sheila... did Nan catch up with you?"

Sheila blinked. "Nan? No. Why?"

Realization crashed into Stone's mind, and he cursed out loud, standing up. His reaction unnerved Raoul, who realized something was wrong. "What is it?"

"Nan was told to come meet you at a restaurant at *Rue du Suquet*. I think she's being set up."

"Oh, no! By Smollett?"

"He wants to get her on her own."

"Jesus… let's go."

4

CHAPTER FOUR

Nan didn't notice the text messages blinking on her phone until she walked back out on the street. As she walked past the entrance to an alleyway, strong arms reached out and grabbed her, a hand clamping over her mouth. "Say one word or scream and I'll gut you right here, bitch."

Oh God no... Duggan. He dragged her backwards down the darkened alleyway, stopping behind a dumpster and slamming her against the wall. Terrified, Nan's body shut down, and she couldn't breathe. She could feel something pressing against her belly—a weapon? Duggan's face was red with anger. "You got me fired."

Nan swallowed hard. "*You* got you fired, Duggan. You're lucky I didn't call the police."

He laughed in her face. "Hard to testify when you're dead, pretty girl."

Now she felt the sharp tip of the knife he was pressing against her. "You kill me, you go to jail forever. Plenty of people know what you did to me, Duggan."

"Like they're going to think this isn't just a thrill kill. Beautiful girl on her own, found raped, robbed and stabbed to death?

There's one a week, baby girl, and they won't even bother to look into your murder."

"You really going to kill me, Duggan? You want that to be your legacy?" The knife was really cutting into her skin now, tearing through the fabric of her white dress. He would only have to apply a little more pressure and it would sink deep into her soft, vulnerable flesh.

For a long moment, time stopped, and then he smiled. "Yes, I really do. Bye bye, beautiful."

Nan closed her eyes and waited to die.

Then she gasped as the knife was ripped away from her, and she opened her eyes to see Stone Vanderberg pick Duggan up and smash him to the ground, pummeling the man. Sheila and Raoul were close behind him, Sheila going to Nan and wrapping her arms around her. Raoul helped Stone drag Duggan toward the street as a couple of gendarmes came running.

AFTER NAN WAS QUESTIONED for hours, they finally allowed her to go get checked out at a hospital. She objected but Stone, Sheila, and Raoul all insisted. Duggan was arrested. "He doesn't see the light of day," Stone had sternly ordered the police sergeant.

Eventually, as dawn broke, all four went back to the Carlton. Word had spread about the attempted murder, and Nan found the stares of the hotel staff intrusive and upsetting. Sheila kissed her cheek. "Baby girl, rest. Call me when you're ready. I'm so, so sorry."

Nan saw Stone and Raoul exchange a loaded glance, and Raoul came to hug her. "My flight is in a couple of hours, but I can cancel."

"No, please, I'm fine," she said but hugged him hard. She heard him give a little sob.

"I'm so sorry, Nook."

She knew he was devastated about what happened. He had known how Etta's rape and suicide had scarred her, and now that this had happened, Nan knew Raoul would dwell on it. "Owl, I'm okay, I promise."

He studied her, then nodded at Stone. "Don't be too much of a feminist to not let Mr. Vanderberg look out after you."

Nan chuckled. "Still matchmaking."

"Always. I love you, Nook."

"Love you, too, Owl."

FINALLY, alone in her suite, they sat together on the couch. Nan smiled at Stone. "This was a really strange way of getting to know each other."

Stone grinned. "I'm just glad you're okay." He looked down at her dress, and his smile faded. There was a patch of blood that had seeped from the tiny cut Duggan's knife made. "My God."

Nan flushed and covered the spot with her hand. "I'm okay."

Stone gazed at her in silence for a long moment, then he slowly leaned in and pressed his lips to hers. The kiss was soft and brief, but it left her lips tingling. "Stone?"

"Yes, baby?"

She stroked his face. "How about we take this dress off and throw it in the trash?"

His smile was wide. "I like that idea." He got up and offered her his hand, which she took, standing up to meet him. He drew her into his arms and kissed her, his fingers gently drawing the zipper on the back of her dress down, tantalizingly slow, until she was desperate for him to rip the dress from her.

But he knew what he was doing—that was clear enough. Slowly, he slipped the dress from her shoulders, trailing his lips along her throat to her shoulder, then as he drew the dress down lower, he freed her breast from the lacy cup of her bra and took her nipple in his mouth. Nan gasped and caught her bottom lip in her teeth as his tongue flicked around the small nub. His hands were on her waist, stroking the soft skin, before his fingers tightened firmly onto her flesh as he pulled her closer, his desire becoming animal.

Nan could have screamed when his mouth left her nipple, but, grinning, Stone swept her up into his arms and carried her to the bedroom. "God, you're a beautiful woman," he murmured as he pulled her dress off and laid her down. His fingers snagged the sides of her panties as he swiftly drew them down her legs, and then he was hitching her legs over his shoulders. The second his tongue lashed around her clit, Nan knew that this was going to be the most erotic night of her life. Stone teased and flicked his tongue so expertly, that when he finally plunged his tongue deep into her cunt, Nan cried out and came almost immediately, shivering and trembling, all control lost.

Stone's lips found her mouth as she was tearing at his shirt, desperate to run her hands over his hard body. The thickly muscled arms and shoulders she revealed were powerful and rock hard.

Nan took his nipple into her mouth and worked her tongue around it, pleased when she heard his groan of arousal. Stone expertly kicked off his pants and underwear, and Nan stroked his huge, thick cock against her belly. His eyes were soft. "I've been thinking about this for so long…"

"I want you inside me," Nan whispered, her shyness overwhelmed by her desire for him, and he nodded. He reached down to his pants, pulling a condom out of his back pocket. Nan grinned.

"Why do I think you're always prepared?"

Stone chuckled, and she was glad he was good-humored during sex—there was nothing worse than a po-faced lover.

But Stone was anything but stone-faced. He smiled down at her, brushing his lips over hers. "Nanouk...." He thrust into her, and she gave a sharp intake of breath as he filled her entirely.

She moaned with pleasure, and Stone gathered her to him as they moved together. "Wrap your legs around me, beautiful. Let me in deeper."

She obeyed him, tilting her hips up to meet his, squeezing her thighs around his waist as they fucked. Stone kissed her, pouring every bit of desire he felt into his kiss. The way his eyes held hers made Nan feel like the most beautiful thing in the world at that moment.

Their bodies fit together perfectly, despite the difference in height. Her belly pressed against his; her breasts crushed against his rock-hard chest. His cock, thick, long and powerful reamed into her swollen, sensitive cunt, and Nan cried out as her orgasm hit, arching her back. Stone groaned and came, too, his lips against her throat, his cock pumping hard.

They collapsed back on the bed together, and Stone quickly and gently excused himself to deal with the used condom. Nan tried to catch her breath, her body feeling strange as if it wasn't hers. Stone returned and lay down beside her, drawing her close. Nan nuzzled close to his immense size and warmth. In his arms, she felt safe, she realized—something she hadn't felt for a long time.

"Are you okay?" Stone asked, his voice tender, and she smiled up at him.

"More than okay... that was incredible."

He chuckled. "Yes, it was..." They gazed at each other for a long time, then Stone pressed his lips to hers. "Nan Songbird... do you get into Manhattan often? For reasons other than work, I mean."

Nan smiled. "You don't have to do that, Stone. I know the

rules men like you play by, and it's okay. I'm not asking for anything from you than this moment here."

Stone blinked. "I meant what I said... I'd like to see you again."

She studied his expression—he seemed genuine, and a flush of pleasure ran through her. "Really?"

His chuckle was soft. "Really. I know my reputation, Nan, and believe me, I've more than lived up to it. But... this feels different. Don't you feel that, too?"

Slowly she nodded. "I do... but then I don't have a great deal to compare it with."

Stone looked confused. "What do you mean?"

Nan said nothing but held his gaze, watching understanding —and then shock—creep into his expression.

"No *way*," he said softly.

It was her turn to laugh. "Yes, *way*. I was a virgin."

"Holy fuck."

Her mouth hitched up in a grin. "Well, it was kind of biblical, yes." Stone laughed, but his eyes still registered confusion.

"No, seriously, Nan. You were a virgin?"

"I know, in this day and age, it's crazy. But I never felt the urge to make love to anyone before now. I guess that's kind of fucked up—I'm twenty-eight years old, but things happened when I was younger. My sister was raped. It had an effect." Nan had no idea why she was telling this man all of this, but she wanted him to understand her: why she had held back on losing her virginity and why she had finally chosen the person to give it to. She felt anxiety for the first time as she waited for his reply.

"Sweet Nan... my God, you're just... unique," Stone shook his head, and she felt his arms tighten around her. "Thank you for the honor... God, that sounds weird, but I mean it."

She smiled at him. "But it doesn't mean you owe me anything. That's what I'm getting at. I know the way the world works, and how someone powerful and desirable works. I'm not a little girl."

"Nanouk Songbird, can I get a word in?" Stone was laughing now, and she had to giggle at his expression.

"Sure, sorry."

"For one thing, stop apologizing. For another... can we just see where this goes? For once in my life, I have a woman in my arms who, for want of a better word, isn't interested in *Stone Vanderberg*—his money, position, society, or any of that bullshit. I knew that about you the first time I saw you, and you shut down Sheila's interview. You had my number, and I cannot tell you how thrilling that is to me. You're a challenge, and God knows, I need that in my life. For years, I admit—I've screwed my way around the globe and had a fantastic time doing it. Beautiful women are two-a-penny, Nan, although they pale in comparison to you."

Nan flushed at the compliment. "But?"

"But none of them have had the potential to be more than a fuck-buddy," he said, honestly. "But with you... there's a possibility I've found something extra, something I didn't know I was looking for until now."

Nan's emotions were in turmoil. "What? What are you looking for?"

Stone's handsome face was soft. "A best friend," he said simply, and Nan's eyes filled with tears.

"Really?"

Stone nodded, drawing her closer and kissing her. "Really." And they began to make love again.

5

CHAPTER FIVE

A week later and the film festival was coming to a close. Sheila Maffey had taken home the Best Actress award and was throwing a party for her fellow cast and crew. She had insisted on Nan inviting Stone and Nan being off duty for the night.

"Have a relaxing time, darling. You've been my rock here—you really have." Sheila nodded toward Stone who was talking to some of the crew. "And Stone Vanderberg is crazy about you, that's obvious."

Nan had flushed, but she had to admit—it really did seem like Stone was happy. He looked up now; his gaze going directly over to her and leaving her with a wink. He was so tall that he towered over most of the other guests. *My lover, my friend.* The past week had passed in a delirious whirl of love-making and talking and laughing, and now she couldn't imagine a time when she hadn't known this man.

Tomorrow, after the Festival closed, Stone intended to take her to his private villa in Antibes. He had persuaded Nan to take a week's vacation. "Just so we can really have some time to ourselves before we get back to our real lives—we can figure out how to make this work."

Nan had said yes without hesitating. As the party drew to a close, Stone appeared back by her side and took her hand. "Shall we?"

Her heart was pounding as they drove through the night, the top of Stone's rented Mercedes down. Nan let her long hair fly free, and Stone grinned at her as she tried to control it. Nan gave up in the end, and by the time Stone parked the car outside the villa, her hair was a mess of tangled waves. "Shot," Nan said, trying to tame it. "How come in the movies that's supposed to be sexy and yet in real life, I just end up looking like a Wookie?"

Stone burst out laughing. "Yeah, but, *sexy* Wookie."

Nan grinned. She had discovered that Stone shared the same goofy sense of humor as her—something she would never have expected. His outward appearance was so together, sometime even severe in his masculinity, that Nan was surprised when he could be as kid-like and silly as she was. There was a twelve-year age gap, but she never felt it once.

Now, he took her hand as they entered the warmly lit villa. "Are there other people here?"

Stone shook his head. "I asked the staff to prepare the house but other than that... it's just the two of us." His voice had dropped to a sensual purr and Nan shivered with anticipation.

"So, you have me all alone for a week."

"What *shall* we do?" Stone grinned as he drew her into his arms. Nan pressed her body against his.

"I can think of a few things..."

With a growl, he swept her up into his arms and carried her as she giggled furiously into the villa. They didn't make it as far as the bedroom before they were ripping each other's clothes off.

They made love on the cool tile floor, ignoring the hard ground as they fucked with abandon.

THE NEXT MORNING, Nan slowly woke, laying on her stomach, feeling Stone's fingertips drawing up and down her spine. She opened her eyes and smiled at him. His delicious navy eyes were soft with adoration. "Waking up with you, Nan Songbird, is the perfect way to begin a day."

"Right back at you, handsome." Nan couldn't believe how comfortable she was with this man—this man whose family and status were so far above her own humble background.

But here, in this Mediterranean paradise, she could pretend that they were just two people enjoying a passionate, fun affair, and that the outside world or their lives had no bearing on it.

The sex was incredible. Stone was a tender but masterful lover, and he made Nan curious to be more adventurous. When she told him that, Stone smiled. "We can be as adventurous as you like, baby."

After dinner one night in the old town, Stone led her down the old stone streets of the city, and he fucked her against a stone wall down a dark side alley as people passed by the street end, his hand over her mouth to stifle her cries of pleasure. The thrill of almost being caught infected her, and Nan knew she would be open to trying anything with this man. She didn't want to think about going back to the States and have the real world intrude into her little bubble.

It wasn't just the sex either. They talked about their families. Stone told her about his brother Ted, who managed Eliso's career as well as other major movie stars and his parents who were loving but kept themselves to themselves in their Oyster Bay mansion.

"Are you and Ted close?"

Stone nodded. "We are—the best of friends. We had a sister, Janie. She died when she was only five."

"Oh God, how awful, I'm so sorry. Was she sick?"

Stone shook his head. "She drowned in the ocean next to our property. Ted was with her. I don't think he's ever forgiven himself, even though he was only a kid himself."

"Poor thing." Nan sighed. "So much pain."

"You mentioned your sister."

Nan nodded. "Etta was everything to me and when she died..."

"I know." Stone cupped her cheek in his hand. "You're not alone anymore."

Nan swallowed hard and looked away. "Don't promise anything, Stone. I just ask that. Don't promise anything."

THEY TALKED ABOUT THEIR DREAMS. Stone and Nan shared a love for their respective jobs. "When I go back to New York," Nan told him, "I'm finally going to be able to work in the criminal law realm. I'm so excited—I can't even tell you."

Stone grinned at her. "I can tell. What is it about criminal law?"

"I like puzzles, especially when it comes to human motivation," she said, honestly. "I think it stems from my sister's suicide, to be honest...the thought processes behind people's actions."

"But you'll be working for a defense lawyer?"

Nan nodded. "The experience will be invaluable, and Alan is taking a risk taking on someone like me. So, eventually, yeah, I'd like to prosecute and get rapists off the street, but it's always useful to see the other side of it, too."

Stone studied her. "Playing devil's advocate...?"

Nan smiled. "Go on."

"How do you not let Etta's situation color your attitude to the defendants?"

Nan sat up. "That is a very good question, and I've asked myself that over and over. If I ever thought I couldn't put my personal feelings aside, I would recuse myself from the case."

Stone nodded but stayed silent. Nan studied his expression. "You don't think I could do it?"

"I would never say you were incapable of anything. I just can see how passionate you are about things."

Nan grinned and wriggled into his arms. "You're biased."

Stone kissed her, tightening his arms around her. "I admit I am."

"So, you know about my Achilles' heel... what's yours?"

Stone hesitated. "You really want to know?"

"Of course."

He drew in a deep breath. "Kids."

"Kids?"

He nodded. "It's probably why I've gotten to forty and never been married. Kids. I don't want them. Seeing my parent's grief after Janie died... it's that thing that terrifies me—losing something, or someone, I loved again."

Nan was a little shocked. "Stone, we all lose people."

"I know, and I also know it's foolish to try to minimize personal loss. I'm reconciled to the fact that my parents will die and my brother someday. It's the reason I've never gotten close to someone."

Nan nodded but was quiet for a long time after. It hurt to think that yes, this little period of time with Stone was temporary, but they had both known that, hadn't they? It hurt to hear it out loud though.

STONE NOTICED Nan was quieter after their talk and wondered if he had hurt her feelings. At dinner, over Stone's signature pan-seared sirloin and salad on the terrace of the villa, he took her hand. "What I said, Nan... I didn't mean *us*. Although I don't know what 'us' means at this point."

"Let's just enjoy this week," she said, smiling at him. "We said no promises."

"We did. But I would like to see where this goes. I understand if you have reservations. There's a significant age gap between us, after all."

"That's not an issue, but... God, I don't know, Stone. I'm new to all of this. I don't know how to do it." Nan looked away from him, and he was horrified to see tears in her eyes.

"Hey, hey, hey," he said softly, stroking her hair. "Don't cry, baby, it's okay. Let's just enjoy ourselves these last few days."

LATER, as she lay naked in his bed, Stone took her hand and turned it palm-side up, then kissed the inside of her wrist softly. "Nanouk Songbird, you have enchanted me." He trailed his lips up her arm, along her shoulder to her throat. Nan wrapped her legs around his hips, gazing up at him, as his mouth found hers.

His dark eyes crinkled at the edges as he smiled down at her, and his cock plunged deep inside her. Would she ever get enough of this man? His big, powerful body dominated hers so entirely when they were fucking, and she knew, to her regret, that she would never get a better man in her bed. *Oh, damn it, oh damn it.* Nan knew she was falling for him and the thought terrified her. She knew, once they were out of their Antibes bubble, every small difference in their lives would begin to create cracks —and the thought of it made her chest hurt.

No. Focus. Focus on these few days and make them the best days of your life.

So, they swam in the warm ocean, explored the old town, ate

at incredible restaurants, went dancing in sultry nightclubs and made love endlessly. Stone made her laugh constantly. The sight of this huge mountain of a man goofing off like a teenager warmed her heart and made it even harder to contemplate the end of their fling.

IT WAS the eve of their last day, and they had returned from a day trip to Monaco, exhausted and hungry. They grabbed dinner at a small café in the old town, and then walked slowly back to the villa. Both of them were quiet, their fingers entwined, knowing that soon, they would be flying back to New York and their real lives.

In the bedroom Stone left the light off, a full moon casting an ethereal cast into the room. He pulled slowly at the belt of her dress and peeled it from her shoulders, wanting to look at Nan in the moonlight. Her soft beauty killed him: her large chocolaty brown eyes gazing up at him, the soft blush of her caramel skin. "There isn't a more beautiful sight in the world than you, Nan Songbird, at this moment."

She blinked slowly at him, her mouth curving up in a shy smile, but she remained silent. He freed her breasts from her bra and drew her panties down her legs. For such a petite woman, her legs went on for days, shapely and toned. Stone drew his fingers down her belly, splaying his fingers out over the soft curve of it. He dropped to his knees and buried his face in it, his tongue tracing a pattern around her deep navel.

He felt her tremble as his fingers trailed up her inner thigh, stopping before they touched her hot sex. He teased her, stroking every part of her, but never touching her groin. Stone gazed up at her. "Open these beautiful legs for me, my darling."

Nan shivered as she obeyed him, and he grinned. "I have an idea. Do you trust me?"

She nodded, and he stood, scooping her up and carrying her into the kitchen before sitting her down on a wooden chair. "Wait here."

In the bedroom he snagged a couple of his neck ties and took them back to the kitchen. "You want to stop, just say it," he told her as he wound the tie around her eyes, then bound her hands behind her. "This is supposed to be fun, to be exciting, but if you get scared…"

"I won't." Nan grinned and spread her legs slowly and he could see how excited, how wet she was for him. Stone smiled. He knelt down and licked her cunt, making her shiver. "That's just a tiny preview, baby."

Stone grabbed an ice cube, and putting it in his mouth, trailed it from her throat down to her navel. Two fingers on his left hand slid inside her slick cunt as his thumb stroked a rhythm on her clit. With the ice cube on his tongue, he took each of her nipples into his mouth in turn and teased each nubbin until Nan was writhing on the chair, the pleasure clearly almost unbearable. Her sex flooded with moisture, soaking his hand, and Stone felt triumphant. He trailed the ice cube down her stomach again and circled it around her navel, then downward, licking it into her sex as she moaned her excitement.

Her clit reacted to his tongue, hardening and pulsing with desire. The ice cube melted quickly, and he buried his face in her sex, his tongue plunging deep inside in quick, sharp jabs until Nan cried out, coming, her entire body trembling and drenched in sweat.

Stone smiled and moved up to kiss her mouth. "Can you taste yourself on me, beauty? You taste like honey." He kissed her thoroughly, his tongue lashing around hers. "Nan?"

"Yes?" She was breathless, utterly under his control.

"I'm going to fuck you until you weep, pretty girl."

She moaned, and it was such a magical sound to him that

he was desperate to be inside her. He unzipped and freed his cock, straining and throbbing, and quickly releasing her hands, he tumbled her, still blindfolded, to the floor. Nan giggled then gasped as he thrust into her hard, his hands pinning hers to the carpet, his powerful legs spreading hers wide, his thighs heavy on hers. "Tell me you're mine, Nanouk Songbird..."

"I'm yours," she whispered, her voice breaking a little, "I'm yours, Stone..."

Stone slammed his hips harder and harder against hers, making her cunt pulse and convulse around his cock. Their breath mingled, their kisses wet and animalistic, hungry for each other.

Nan could feel an explosive orgasm building, every cell in her body on fire and when it hit her, it felt as if she would die, completely taken out of her own body and soaring into the heavens. Stone was relentless even as she cried out. He tore the blindfold from her eyes, and she gazed into his navy eyes, which seemed black, full of desire and danger.

I could die right here, she thought, *and it would be okay with me.* The passion she felt and the feral desire in his eyes frightened her a little. The force of her feelings for this man scared her.

"You drive me crazy," Stone growled at her as he too came, his cock spasming as it pumped out his cum. Nanouk felt the power of it releasing inside her—did the condom break?

She saw in Stone's eyes that he was thinking the same thing. "It's okay," she said softly, "I'm on birth control."

The relief she saw in his eyes gave her a strange pain that she couldn't understand. He kissed her tenderly now as if she were the most precious woman he had ever held in his arms, and she knew that couldn't be true.

As he gathered her into his warm embrace, her head against his hard chest, Nan suddenly felt tearful. This was all illusion—

a beautiful illusion, yes—but there was no way it would survive outside this week.

Just enjoy it, don't dwell. But she felt as if she could cry and never stop. *Fuck.* Wasn't this feeling what she had run away from all her life? And all in less than a week, she had destroyed her peace of mind for what? She looked up into the eyes of the man she had given herself to and felt a rising panic. *I'm lost,* she thought, and *it's going to hurt like hell to say goodbye.* Stone was watching her, his eyes curious, seeing her turmoil.

"What is it, baby?" His voice was soft, full of love, of compassion, but she just shook her head.

"Nothing. Just hold me, please."

STONE WAITED until Nan had fallen into a fitful sleep, and then slipped from the bed, standing at the end of it for a second to watch her sleep. He didn't want to think about tomorrow, but his life was way too complicated for him to ask her to share it. Nanouk deserved better than a part-time lover, and Stone knew as well, that he too had to step away before he fell too deep.

Because Nanouk would be very easy to fall in love with—very, *very* easy—Stone told himself fiercely that he wasn't in love already, but he knew it to be a lie, and he couldn't handle it. What if he hurt her? She was too good for him—he knew that. She deserved a protector, a champion, an equal, and Stone Vanderberg, for the first time in his life, knew he wasn't enough for her.

God, the thought of not being able to see her, touch her, make love to her after today was killing him, and that's why he knew he had to end things. They had promised each other until tomorrow, and as much as it would hurt, he would keep to that.

He went into the kitchen and grabbed a glass of ice cold

water for his parched throat. Stone closed his eyes. *Don't fall for her, but don't waste a single second that she could be in your arms.*

He went back to bed and gathered her into his arms. Nan opened her dark brown eyes and smiled at him sleepily, and slowly they began to make love, knowing it may be the last time.

IN THE MORNING, he woke, and Nan was gone.

CHAPTER SIX

-NEWYORK

ne year later...

ALAN ELIZONDO SMILED at his junior attorney at law as they prepared to meet their latest client. "Are you excited?"

Nan nodded at him, her stomach churning with both anticipation and trepidation. "It's just ironic, is all. I spend years trying to escape entertainment law, and my first big criminal case is defending a movie star."

Alan chuckled. "Nan, it's just the way the cookie crumbles. Eliso Patini is an innocent man, whether he's a movie star or not."

"You're convinced of his innocence."

Alan nodded. They were sitting in Alan's vast conference room in his Manhattan office, awaiting the arrival of their client and his entourage. The shock news that Eliso had been accused of the murder of a fan had reverberated around the globe a few days earlier, and when Alan had told Nan that Eliso had hired his firm to represent him in court, Nan had sighed. Another reminder, as if she needed it, of Stone Vanderberg. It seemed as if, even after a year, she couldn't escape mention of the man whose bed she had left in the early hours of a May morning a year ago.

She shook the thought away. "If it's one thing I learned about movie stars it's that they have a tendency to turn up with a fleet of Yes Men, so I'm anticipating we may need to press our points home."

"Good info." Alan sat back in his chair. "I'm hoping you will take the lead on this, Nan, so I'm going to be looking at your reaction to talking truth to power."

"Fair enough. I almost met Patini last year in Cannes, actually."

"Almost?"

Nan grinned. "I was invited to join him and his friends for lunch... but I settled for Owl instead."

Alan laughed loudly. "I see."

There was a knock at the door and Michael, Alan's uber-efficient P.A., stuck his head in the door. "Mr. Patini is here."

"Send them up. Thanks, Michael."

"How big is his team?" Nan asked Michael before he disappeared.

"Oh, huge," Michael said, with a mischievous grin and chuckle as he closed the door.

A few moments later, Nan and Alan stood as Eliso Patini with his long-term lover Beulah—and no one else—came into the room. The actor, achingly handsome with his dark curls and bright green eyes, looked exhausted and bewildered as he shook hands with Alan, then Nan. Beulah, beautiful and exotic, said hello; her eyes registering recognition when she looked at Nan, and smiled at her.

Nan nodded back. Despite her professionalism, her heart

went out to the young couple who both looked devastated at the situation.

"Eliso," Alan started, his voice warm and empathetic, "why don't you tell us what happened?"

Eliso rubbed his face, dark circles under his eyes. "This is how I experienced things, so if there is any difference with the actual truth, I know nothing about it."

"Fair enough. I want to hear it from you."

Eliso sighed. "Last Monday night, Beulah and I were at a charity function on the Upper East Side—a benefit for an AIDS charity I've been working closely with since my brother died. There were a lot of my fans there, fans who had paid extraordinary amounts to be there, and I wanted to make sure each of them was rewarded for their generosity. So, we had a group cocktail session before the benefit and a meet and greet."

Beulah joined in. "Eli's more than generous with his time, and so, the meet and greet went on for three, four hours. Most of the fans were more than happy—they got personal time, they got things signed, they had a great time. It wasn't until the last group where things got... strange." Beulah tucked her hand into Eliso's, and Nan felt warmth towards the other woman. She was here to support her man, and Nan found it touching.

"Define *strange*." Alan was scratching notes out on a legal pad.

"There was a young woman, a dark-haired girl, who didn't seem to... God, this is going to sound so wrong, but it didn't seem as if she would have had the money to be there." Beulah made a face at her words. "Sorry, I don't mean to sound elitist."

"But it's the truth," Eliso said, in his low, mellifluous Italian accent. "And it wasn't just that... her behavior was unsettling. Mr. Elizondo, Ms. Songbird, I've had stalkers before—fans that cross the line. This wasn't like that. She stared at me as if... God, I don't know how to describe it."

"As if she hated him," Beulah finished for him. "And... she had track marks. I saw them even though she covered her arms up quickly. Then, out of nowhere, she started to scream."

Goosebumps raised on Nan's skin, and she shivered involuntarily. Both Eliso and Beulah saw her, and Beulah nodded. "Yes, exactly that. It was so shocking. She screamed and went for Eliso. You see the scratches on his face."

"My protection pulled her away, but before they could throw her out, she shouted at me that I would 'pay' for what I had done to her." Eliso closed her eyes and shook his head, looking sick. "I swear to both of you, to Beulah, I never saw the girl before in my life. *Ever*."

Beulah looked bleak. "The next morning, the police came. The girl had been found stabbed to death in an alleyway behind our hotel. They found a knife."

"A knife that they swear has a man's DNA on it." Eliso finished, his whole body slumping in defeat. "I, of course, offered a sample immediately. There's no way it will match mine. I swear on my father's grave... I did not kill that girl, and I have no idea why she attacked me. The police found a journal which they say details a year-long affair between the two of us which ended in an abortion. Of course, it's the work of a fantasist, but here's the thing... she knew things she couldn't have possibly known about me, about my life."

"And the DA is using that as enough evidence to proceed with a trial?"

Eliso nodded. "He is... I think he is also looking to raise his personal profile, but maybe that's me just being bitter."

"It wouldn't be unheard of," Alan nodded, but Nan frowned.

"Mr. Patini..."

"Eliso, please." He looked her, and she saw a flash of recognition in his eyes. "We've met before?"

"Almost. A year ago, in Cannes." *Don't talk about Stone, please.* "We nodded at each other in the Grand Salon in the Carlton."

"Oh yes. Well, it's nice to see you again, even under these circumstances."

Nan smiled. "You, too. Both of you. But I have to ask—this seems like someone is setting you up, so are you prepared to talk to us about your relationships and be totally open?"

"One hundred percent," he said, and Nan believed him. This man looked shattered.

"Good," Alan said, and nodded at Nan approvingly. She'd pleased him with that line of questioning. "Look, we'll get refreshments in. Do you have the time to start now?"

Eliso and Beulah nodded. "Whatever it takes."

THEY TALKED FOR HOURS, and Nan was pleased that when Eliso described his friendship with Stone Vanderberg, she managed to stay professional and keep her expression neutral—although she felt Beulah studying her whenever the man's name was mentioned. She was grateful the other woman didn't say anything, though. This wasn't about her or Stone now.

Eliso and Beulah left around six P.M., and Alan looked at his younger associate. "What do you think?"

"I think we need to do everything we can to help that man." Nan nodded at her boss, and Alan smiled.

"I agree. The DA must be crazy—the evidence is flimsy at best, even the DNA. If it's this obvious to us that Patini is being framed, why the hell would the DA pursue this?"

"We need to find out who is setting Eliso up and fast, before his whole life is destroyed." Nan glanced at the clock. "Damn. Look, Al..."

"Go, it's okay, I'm sorry I forgot the time."

Nan smiled at her boss. "You realize you're the best, right?"

"Oh, I know," Alan chuckled as he gathered his papers up. "Look, can I call later? Talk through some stuff?"

"Absolutely."

Nan took the train back to Oyster Bay, her mind whirling with ideas about Eliso's case. She liked the man and his stunning girlfriend immensely and wanted to help them. God, she loved her job: the exhilaration, the tension, the adrenaline. Both Nan and her colleagues had discovered over the last year how tenacious she could be when she got the bit between her teeth—it had surprised Nan, but she knew she had finally found her vocation. Alan was picky whose case he took; he lived on his gut instinct that his clients were innocent of their crimes, and his success rate was so high that he was the obvious choice for people accused wrongly.

Nan respected the fact he took cases on merit and not on how much money or attention they would bring to his practice.

The train rolled to a stop, and she stepped off into the warm evening, Nan switched from work mode to home mode, and to the little girl waiting for at the childminder's home.

Carrie grinned at her as she apologized for being late. "Don't worry about it. She's been an angel."

She handed Nan the three-month-old baby, who gazed up her mother with the dark navy eyes she had inherited from her father. *Ettie. Little Ettie.* Named after her sister, and without a doubt since her birth, the love of Nan's life.

Her daughter…Stone Vanderberg's daughter…

CHAPTER SEVEN

Stone called Eliso later that night. "How did it go?"

"Good, I think. Elizondo is a savvy guy." Eliso sounded tired and drained. "God, Stone, how the fuck did I let this happen?"

"You didn't let anything happen, buddy. Someone is fucking with you." Stone hesitated. "Did you see her?"

"If you mean the lovely Ms. Songbird, then yes." Eliso chuckled softly. "I think having her on my side will be a good thing, too. She seems capable and tenacious."

Stone held back on asking anything more. After all, this was about proving Eliso's innocence, not the woman Stone had been thinking about every moment since she had left his bed last May. "Listen, dude, everyone is behind you. Me, Ted, Fen. All of us."

"I know and don't think I'm not grateful. Listen, I'm so sick of talking about this. How's the magazine coming along?"

For the last year, Stone had been working on publishing his own magazine, a small venture to compliment his already growing stature in the publishing world. Focusing on his hometown of Oyster Bay, he drew attention to the lives of Long Islanders. He had been working on the small press magazine for months now, but Stone, of late, had felt stuck. Why was he doing this, really? He hadn't even been back to Oyster Bay for a while now, and he told himself it was because his life was in Manhattan and not in the tiny hamlet on the north shore of Long Island.

But he had felt that it, in some way, brought him a connection to Nan, however tenuous, and it gave him a little comfort. When she left him that day, he had known she had done the right thing for both of them, but he couldn't get her out of his head. It had taken every ounce of strength not to pursue her, to go with his life, but he had done it.

He'd even slept with a few women, tried to get back into his routine of love 'em and leave 'em, but his heart wasn't in it.

He chatted with Eliso for a few minutes and then hung up. Glancing at the clock, he wondered if he should go out, have a few drinks... and try not to drive out to Long Island. *You don't even know where she lives,* he thought to himself. Not that finding out would be a problem—his family retained enough private detectives that no one was untraceable for the Vanderbergs.

A year. Should he risk catching up with her? Would it really be that dangerous? After all, if Eliso's case went to trial, he and Nan would see each other—why not make the inevitable a little easier by reconnecting in private beforehand?

Satisfied he had a good reason to contact her again, he called one of his most trusted detectives and asked him to find out where she lived on the island. If he could 'accidentally' run into her, all the better.

Stone went out for a drink, buoyed by his decision, and a couple of hours later, he was at a young woman's apartment, having sex with a girl whose name he didn't know. It was a mistake, and he felt bad when it was over, and the girl had tears in her eyes. "I'm so sorry, sweetheart."

On his drive back to his apartment, he felt awful and berated himself for being so reckless with another woman's heart when his own lay with that beautiful woman in Oyster Bay.

"Fuck this shit." Stone shook his head. Why was he messing around when he already knew his heart was taken? *Grow the fuck up, Vanderberg, and go tell Nan how you feel about her, that not being with her is killing you. Do it.*

His mind made up, he felt happier, and when his private detective came through for him with Nan's address, he knew he was doing the right thing. He guessed that she was a workaholic, so he figured Sunday was the best day to seek her out. That gave him three days to prepare himself, but one thing he knew for sure.

He was going to get Nanouk Songbird back in his life.

Eliso Patini hugged his sister, Fenella. "Fen, I'm sorry about all of this."

The dark-haired woman studied her younger brother carefully. "Eli... you look tired."

"I am. I'm not sleeping so good." Eliso saw Fenella shoot a look at Beulah, who gazed back at her without reaction. It bugged him that Fen and Beulah didn't get along well, but right now, he needed both of them.

They were staying at an upscale hotel in Manhattan, and Fen had just arrived from Rome that morning. After collecting Fen from the airport, they had all met with Eliso's legal team again, Fen grilling each member of the team—her anxiety about Eliso's position making her combative and a little aggressive. To their credit, both Alan Elizondo and Nan Songbird had held their own against Fen's barrage of questions.

"I want to know more about the DA... why is he prosecuting such a flimsy case?"

Alan had sighed. "He, Miles Kirke, doesn't think it's so flimsy. At least, he intends to make it a case of a rich man trying to get away with murder—in the press at least."

"And the press will try to destroy your life," Nan said, her warm brown eyes sympathetic as she looked at Eliso, "we all know what they are like, which is why we must always, *always* appear above reproach. Answer every invasive question honestly. Take any test. We *know* you're innocent, Eliso, but we have to make it crystal clear to the world—you have nothing to hide. I promise, we will do everything in our power to make this right."

LATER, Fenella had given her brother her verdict. "I liked them, especially that young woman. She had balls. She won't take any crap from this Kirke person."

"I hope not."

"Stone knows Nan Songbird," Beulah said casually, "and he's a good judge of character."

Fen rolled her eyes. "I don't think we should make judgements on someone's character based on Stone Vanderberg's sex life... I'm assuming that's what you mean by *knows*."

Beulah sighed. Fenella had never liked her—Beulah had completely won over Eliso's parents when they had met, but Fen had never been someone who had female friends. Eliso had apologized to Beulah after the first fraught meeting. "She's hard work, my sister, but she means well."

Beulah wasn't so sure. Fen managed to twist everything Beulah said to make her sound stupid, looking down her nose at Beulah's career. At first, Beulah was rankled by it, making sure that Fen knew that Beulah not only was a successful business woman as well as a model, but that she had a master's degree to boot. After she realized Fen had made her mind up about her, Beulah gave up trying to impress her lover's sister and stayed away from her.

Beulah kissed Eliso's temple. "I'm going to take a bath."

She snagged her phone as she went into the bedroom and scrolled through her numbers to find Nan's number. Beulah's friends were all over the world, her family was in the United Kingdom, but here in New York, now that Fen was here, Beulah suddenly felt very lonely. Nan had given them her personal number. "Call anytime, even if you just want to vent."

Beulah's finger hovered over the call button. Despite her admiration for the young lawyer, they didn't *know* each other—even if Beulah knew Stone was still hung up on her. Would it be an invasion of privacy to call Nan and just shoot the breeze?

She pressed the call button and a couple of seconds later, she heard Nan's soft voice saying hello. "Nan? It's Beulah Tegan."

"Hey, how are you?"

"I'm..." Beulah's voice broke. "I'm not so good. I'm scared shitless, to be honest, for Eliso. For what might happen. I just needed someone to talk to. I'm sorry if I'm bothering you."

"Not at all. Listen, do you want to meet up for a coffee in the city tomorrow? I can take a couple of hours if you like."

"Oh, are you sure?" Beulah felt a weight lift from her shoulders. "I don't want to intrude."

"No, really, I'd enjoy it. Say, *Maman* in Soho at noon?"

"Perfect. Thanks so much, Nan, I really appreciate this."

Beulah said goodbye and went to fill the tub. She needed a girl chat and to vent about Fenella to someone. Also, she smiled to herself, it wouldn't hurt to find out where Nan was on the subject of Stone. Maybe, out of all of this stress, something good could come, and she could make Stone happy again. She had seen how miserable he was after Nan had left—even if he tried to cover it with humor. She had said as much to Eliso, who had rolled his eyes and told her to stay out of it, but Beulah decided to ignore that.

What harm could it do, after all?

CHAPTER EIGHT

Stone took the call from his detective and carefully wrote down Nan's address in Oyster Bay. He knew the street—it had small Cape Cod cottages along it and was a quiet, family neighborhood. He wasn't surprised—he didn't figure Nan for someone who lived in a high-end apartment. Not that she wasn't stylish, but that she wasn't someone who needed status symbols to feel like a whole person. He loved that about her.

"God, listen to yourself," he muttered, "You think you know her?"

"Sorry, Stone?"

Stone blinked and looked up. His personal assistant Shanae had poked her head around the door. "Sorry, Nae."

"Just wanted to know if you wanted anything else before I head out for the night?"

He smiled at her. "No, thanks, Nae. Listen, Monday morning, any chance you could get here early? About eight A.M.? I have some things I need to go through before the magazine launches."

"Sure, no problem."

"You're the best. Goodnight."

"Night, boss."

It was so quiet when the office was empty that Stone couldn't stand it, and he got into his car to drive home. As he drove, however, he turned onto the I-495E and headed out on the familiar route to Oyster Bay. Stone pushed any thoughts of impropriety out of his mind and just drove, knowing he had no right to go to Nan's home, but unable to stop himself.

An hour and fifteen minutes later, as dusk fell, he parked the car at the end of her street and got out. The house wasn't hard to find, nestled in its own little patch of trees, set back from the road. The wood-framed house was shabby but obviously well-loved—Stone could imagine Nan painting the wood herself, covered in paint, her dark hair shoved up in a messy bun.

Stone stopped himself. *What the hell, man? Now you're having fantasies about her painting and decorating? Jesus...*

And don't forget, Vanderberg, you are lurking, actually lurking *outside her home... after dark.* Stone blew out his cheeks, and casting a last look back at the house, strode back to his car. Damn, he'd really lost the plot. Stalking an ex-lover? *Nope,* Stone thought to himself, *this isn't going to be my life. Forget her, it's over.*

As he started the car, he saw a Mercedes draw up to Nan's house and a tall, dark-haired man he recognized got out. Raoul Elizondo... he'd met him in Cannes the day Nan was attacked. Stone watched as Elizondo went to her door and knocked then, and when Stone saw her, his heart leapt. Her dark hair was down and past her waist, messy and wavy, soft as she grinned at her friend, her smile lighting up the twilight. Stone's stomach twisted with desire and at that moment, he knew. He couldn't let her go.

Their story wasn't over; he knew it in his bones, deep in his marrow. Whatever had been between them was unfinished, unresolved. Stone watched as Raoul picked her up and twirled her around—Nan's musical laugh made it all the way across the street to his car. He wasn't worried that Elizondo was competition—his own Gaydar was fully functional—but he was envious of the easy way Nan had around the other man. Stone had no idea what that felt like—their coupling, their time together had been fraught with tension—mostly sexual, and then when they both knew their time together was coming to an end, with a haunted desperation to make the most of every moment they had left.

He couldn't look away from the two friends now as they chatted, Raoul pointing out something on her porch that made her laugh and swat at him. He was teasing her. Something like jealousy twisted in Stone's gut, and he was glad for his car's tinted windows when he reversed backwards a little too violently, and they both looked over at him. Stone quickly turned the car around, and sped off away from her neighborhood, cursing the fact he'd come here at all.

He had wanted to answer the question whether he was over Nanouk Songbird and instead came away with a whole new raft of questions, and the gnawing certainty that no, he was nowhere in the region of being over her.

"Recognize the car?" Raoul followed Nan into her house after they watched the dark Lotus scream back down the street.

"Nope, and I doubt he or she was from around here with a car like that. Anyway, who cares? God, it's so good to see you, Owl." Nan hugged him again, then held him at arm's length to study him. "You look... seasoned. Well-traveled."

Raoul grinned. "You mean old and destined for the scrapyard."

"Ha ha, no, you look good. Do I detect the smug air of the recently laid?"

"You might." Raoul chuckled as he followed her into her tiny galley kitchen. "Jeez, Nook. Got a cat to swing?"

Nan grinned at him as she filled a kettle. "It's big enough for us. Some of us can't spend our money travelling the world for a year."

Raoul smiled. "Talking of which... where is my goddaughter? Photographs and Facetime can't compare with actually holding her."

Nan beckoned him to follow her. "The little ratbag is pretending to be asleep, but I know her—she's eavesdropping. She's such a nosy little monster." She grinned as she talked about her daughter. "Come and see. I guarantee, she'll be awake."

Raoul followed her into Ettie's bedroom whereas Nan had predicted, the little girl was awake, smiling, gurgling happily when she saw them.

"You little minx," Nan said fondly and picked her up. Raoul reached out and stroked Ettie's plump little cheek.

"God, Nan, she's the image of you."

Nan grinned at him, and Ettie spit up on her mommy's shoulder then laughed. "See? *Monster*." She bounced Ettie over to Raoul's waiting arms, and then cleaned herself up. Raoul cuddled Ettie who pulled at his beard and stuck her tiny finger up his nose.

"She has no boundaries," Nan chuckled as Raoul pretended to bit Ettie's fingers, "Mommy's boobies are apparently chew toys as well, aren't they, minx? Come on, let's go sit. I have a bottle of wine that needs our attention."

Later, when Ettie was asleep in Raoul's arms and Nan was curled upon the couch next to them, Raoul studied his friend. "What strikes me most," he said, "is coming back after these months away and finding you... content. Motherhood suits you more than I would have ever imagined."

Nan smiled. "I'm not saying it's been easy, but yes. Keeping Ettie was the best decision I ever made. I cannot imagine living my life without her now. Your dad made it so much easier for me to work and have her, too. I owe him everything."

Raoul studied his sleeping goddaughter for a while. "She's precious. Nook…"

"Owl, don't."

"I have to. As a man who hopes someday to be a father… I have to say this. Stone Vanderberg has a right to know."

Nan sighed and looked away, remaining silent. Raoul waited. Finally, she rubbed her face. "Owl, he doesn't want kids, and by that, I don't mean he's so-so about it. He told me—kids are his Achilles' heel. He told me point blank he doesn't want them. When I found out I was pregnant, for the first three months, I ignored it."

"I know. Dad said he'd never had anyone start work for him like you did, like a cruise missile. He knew something was up."

Nan chuckled softly. "Is it weird to say that I wish Alan was my dad? I mean, I loved my parents, don't get me wrong, but your dad understands me in a way mine never did."

"He does that."

Nan leaned over and stroked Ettie's face. "You know he offered me a year's paid maternity leave? I couldn't do it, not even for my little bean. Besides, this is my new normal for the next however many years, and so I thought going straight back to work was the best thing. And I was right. I was lucky, too. I found the best babysitter in the world in my opinion. Carrie's lovely. If you weren't gay, I'd be setting you two up."

"If I weren't gay, I'd be proposing to *you*, Nook, and giving this little girl a father." Raoul's words came out harsher than he obviously meant, and he gave her an apologetic grin. "Not judging, just saying. In fact, Nan, if you want a husband, who cares if I'm gay?"

Nan smiled at him. "You are my best friend and the loveliest, sweetest man in the world, and there's no way I would marry you. Do you really think I'd let you throw your chance of happiness away for my own reasons? Hell, no."

Raoul laughed quietly. "Well, obviously, at our mansion in the Hamptons, I'd have Rodrigo the pool boy to sate my Sapphic needs."

"Isn't Sappho related to lesbians rather than gay men?"

"Potato, potato." Raoul shrugged, and Nan giggled.

"You lunatic. Anyway, thank you for the offer, but we're fine. Besides, Ettie needs an uncle to spoil her—I'm going to be such a disciplinarian."

"God, I can imagine. Ettie will be coming to me for advice about the boys you'll ban her from seeing..."

"I'm keeping her in padlocked dungarees until she's thirty."

"... and wanting to buy her first pair of sexy underwear...."

"Nope. Granny-panties until she's fifty."

Raoul laughed a little too loudly, and Ettie opened her navy-blue eyes. They both waited for her to cry, but instead she smiled and stuck her finger up Raoul's nose again.

"That is a weird habit, little one," he said, gently removing it.

"Maybe she thinks your boogers are made of gold."

"Well, it's the Long Island version of being born with a silver spoon."

Nan giggled at him. "Eww." She sighed. "I'm so happy to see you, Raoul. It has been too, too long. Now, tell me about your vacation... and this mystery new man in your life."

THE MAN who was following Stone noted the address he'd driven to, then returned to his office and looked it up. He hooted with laughter when he saw who lived in the tiny cottage in the working-class neighborhood. Eliso Patini's lawyer. His lawyer!

Why was Patini's best friend rocking up to his lawyer's place in the middle of the evening?

Whatever. Vanderberg's actions had put the girl on his shit list now. He found a photo of her on her firm's website and printed it out, tacking it to the board he had set up. He had to admit, it was a shit list of beautiful people—Patini, his girlfriend, Vanderberg, and this lawyer girl. Nanouk Songbird. What the hell kind of name was that? He wondered idly if he'd kill her the way he had Patini's groupie. It wouldn't bother him. He'd done it before. He'd do it again. He enjoyed it.

His eyes slid back to the actor at the center of all of this. Eliso Patini. He felt a fleeting sympathy for him—he had no idea why this was happening to him, did he? And he never would.

He—and everyone he loved—would be long dead before the truth came out.

CHAPTER NINE

She wasn't prepared at all to see him. The pre-trial session with the judge was supposed to be closed-door, not open to the public, but Nan supposed, when you had as much money and power as Stone Vanderberg's family, you could swing anything.

So, when Stone himself walked into the courtroom the next Monday morning, Nan was hit with a tidal wave of feelings. He didn't look at her until after he'd spoken to Eliso, patted his friend on the back, and kissed Beulah's cheek. Then he turned and looked straight at Nan and never dropped his gaze. She felt her face coloring and was aware of Alan's bemused glance. Taking a deep breath, Nan nodded unsmiling to Stone and turned away, focusing on the judge who was seated now.

OPPOSITE THEM, the district attorney smirked over at them. Dressed in a Saville Row suit, the expensive clothing could not disguise the feral nature of the shark that was Miles Kirke. In his late forties, Miles Kirke had gotten to where he was by treading on everyone and anyone he could. He loved the fame his role brought him as well as the money and the women—the women who had always mocked him in his awkward, geeky teens and twenties before Wayne Kirkland, uber-creep, had transformed himself into the sleek, fast-talking, hard-liner Miles Kirke. His family's money had helped, of course.

Miles had no qualms in ruining his father's business either. His parents—in Kirke's mind, weak liberals—had been broken by his callous nature. Miles had reveled in their despair.

And that's what he loved the most. The wreckage. He'd made it to the DA's office by plotting and scheming to ruin his competition, running rough-shod over the people who helped him rise to the position.

And now he was going to make sure Eliso Patini went to jail for the rest of his life.

ALAN LEANED OVER TO ELISO. "This is a bullshit motion, and the judge knows it. You've already voluntarily forfeited your passport and agreed to stay in a mandated hotel, so Kirke has no reason to ask you to be remanded to jail. Not going to happen. This is purely for the cameras."

"Asshole," Beulah muttered, but Eliso just nodded. Nan felt a rush of empathy towards the dejected man. She shot Miles Kirke a stony look—he smirked back, his eyes running up and down her body. Yep, Beulah was right. *Asshole.*

Nan had met Beulah for coffee the previous Friday, and they had talked about nothing but Eliso and Beulah's worries for him with Nan trying to reassure the other woman that the DA had no case. "We will go to the ends of the earth for him, I swear," she had told the other woman and had been moved when Beulah—so perfect, assured, and confident—had burst into tears. Nan had hugged her hard.

"I'm sorry," Beulah said, after her sobs had ceased. "I can't cry in front of Eli. I have to be strong." She gave Nan a grateful smile. "I can see why he's crazy about you. Stone." Her eyes had widened, shocked at her own words. "I'm sorry, that was inappropriate."

Nan's feelings had been thrown into a turmoil at Beulah's words. *He's crazy about you.* Present tense. Nan had shaken her head, brushed aside the comment, but she'd been thinking about it all weekend. Every time she gazed at her sleeping daughter, she saw Stone in her features. Would he be so 'crazy' about her if he knew the truth?

But now in this courtroom, listening to the judge throw out the DA's motion, she finally let herself feel his presence. Once the court was dismissed, they would all gather outside—and she would speak to the father of her child for the first time in a year. The first time since she left him in Antibes without saying goodbye.

Her mind was telling her to run, but her body ached for him. Even seated at the back of the room, he radiated magnetism. Nan risked a quick glance and met his gaze—and held it.

Oh, shit... I'm in trouble.

AFTER THE HEARING, Miles Kirke—who didn't look at all upset at losing—left immediately to go straight down to the bank of reporters in front of the courthouse. Eliso's security chief came up to them. "Look, they've got all the entrances covered, and they'll take any of you they can get. I think it's best to split up into teams and go separately. My men will take each of you, starting with you, Mr. Patini."

"No, take Beulah first, then Fen and Ms. Songbird..." Eliso, ever the gentlemen, looked determined.

"Fine. Ms. Tegan, come with me."

A big hand closed around Nan's. "Come with me." Stone's

voice was low but firm, and Nan found herself rushed along a corridor and down to the basement parking garage. She saw Beulah and Fen being put into black sedans as Stone practically dragged her to his Lotus—a very *familiar* Lotus.

As Stone drove the car out of the parking garage, Nan looked at him. "You were outside my house last week... the night Raoul was there."

Stone nodded. "I was and I'm sorry. It was an invasion of privacy that was beneath me."

Nan felt her chest tighten, but she couldn't figure out whether it was with anger or with... *delight*. "You wanted to see me."

Stone nodded. "I did. Forgive me, Nan, I know what we said last year but I can't stop thinking about you."

Tell him. Tell him his daughter is waiting to meet her father. Tell him. "Where are we going?"

"My place. We need to talk."

They drove in silence for the few minutes it took to get to his place. In the elevator to his penthouse, they just gazed at each other. As soon as Stone opened the door to his apartment, Nan knew for sure that they wouldn't be doing any talking.

Stone closed the door slowly and then as if no time had passed, drew her into his arms and kissed her gently. Nan kissed him back, feeling how much desire he was pouring into the embrace. Stone plucked out the hairpins that were holding her hair up, and as it tumbled down her back, his lips were at her ear. "Take your clothes off, Nanouk..."

His hands were sliding into her jacket, pulling it from her shoulders and dropping it on the carpet. Nan kicked her shoes off, then Stone was picking her up as she wrapped her legs around him and carried her to his bedroom. Laying her on the vast bed, he tugged her shirt open, and his mouth fixed on her belly, her breasts, and up to her throat. Nan shimmied out of her skirt as Stone released her bra clasp, his lips hungrily closing over a nipple. Nan tugged his sweater over his head, and soon they were both naked, and Stone was hitching her legs around his waist.

"Are you still on birth control?"

Nan nodded, a faint twinge of guilt in her chest, but the moment Stone thrust into her, she forgot everything else.

"Good," he said roughly, "... because I need to feel your flesh on mine. You kept me waiting a year, woman—a year…"

He fucked her hard, and Nan wasn't sure if it was lust, desire, or vengeance, but she didn't care. The way he commanded her body—it was like a blast of fresh, clean water after a drought. She clung to him, digging her nails in, her teeth on his skin, clawing at his back as he plowed her hard, then after she'd come, he flipped her onto her stomach and fucked her ass, driving her onwards to an explosive orgasm.

AFTERWARDS, Nan slid from the bed and began to put her clothes. Stone watched her incredulously. "What are you doing?"

She gave him a soft smile. "I'm supposed to be at work, Stone, defending your friend. As wonderful as this reunion was…"

She held out her hand to him, but Stone pulled her back onto the bed, kissing her. Nan giggled but put her hands flat against his chest and pushed him away. "I'm serious. Eliso is in a lot of trouble."

Stone finally let her up, watching her as she piled her glorious mane of hair back into a semi-tidy bun. "The power suit thing works for you," he said with a grin, and began to dress himself. "Although I prefer you naked."

Nan laughed. "This is... is this really happening? I feel a little heady."

Stone kissed her. "I can't believe you kept me waiting for a year, Nanouk Songbird. Why did you leave?"

Nan looked away from him. "I had to, you know that. What we had in France... it couldn't go on."

"Why? I mean, I thought so too back then, but now," he shook his head, "I can't remember why."

"We're from two different worlds, Stone. You've seen where I live."

"Bullshit. We belong together, and believe me, that's not something I ever thought I would say to anyone. Screw where we came from; it's where we go from here that matters. Can I see you tonight?"

Nan didn't answer for a moment, and when she did, he saw she was trembling. "No. Not yet. Not while I'm on Eliso's defense team. I need to concentrate, and I need there not to be any semblance of... unprofessionalism. I've worked hard for my career, Stone, you must understand that."

Stone nodded but was unhappy. "So, you're saying no?"

"I'm saying *not yet*. Let's just... become friends for now." She grinned at him. "With the occasional afternoon like this, maybe. I'm only human, after all."

Stone wasn't satisfied with fragments of Nan—he wanted all in, right now, but he understood where she was coming from. "I guess I'll have to settle for that for now, but I warn you, Nan. I'll want more as soon as the case is over."

"And we'll talk about it then." She sat down next to him on the bed. "It's not that I don't want you, Stone. I do—so, so much, but it's complicated."

Stone gazed at her. God, she was so beautiful it made him want to cry—and she was defending his best friend. "Just... don't leave again without telling me why. I'm too... in this."

Nan cupped his cheek in her hand. "I won't."

"No more secrets."

He saw something flit across her expression but couldn't work it out. Nan kissed him slowly, passionately, and then leaned her forehead against this. "I hate to ask... but could you give me a ride to work please?"

Stone nodded, smiling, but all the way to her office, one thought kept nagging at his brain.

She's hiding something...

CHAPTER TEN

A week later, Nan knocked on Alan's door. "Can I have a word?"

"Sure thing. Have a seat." Alan sat back in his chair and studied her. "You okay? You look pale."

Nan gave him a wry smile. "Lack of sleep, but all in a good cause."

"Ettie?"

"No, no, she's a dream baby, sleeps right through. But this case... something has been bothering me for a while. It was something Beulah said about the victim. That she didn't look like she had the money to be at one of the studio's meet-and-greets. So, I did some digging. I think I've found someone who witnessed the attack. I wanted your permission to go and interview her and then go to the police if I find anything."

"What do you expect to find?"

"What I *hope* to find is proof that someone paid her to attack Eliso."

Alan nodded. "Okay... but Nan, think about this. You could be putting yourself into danger if someone is playing puppet master."

"I know, but I think we need to do this. It could mean the difference between Eliso's freedom or not."

"Fine. Listen, interview the girl then take the rest of the day. You do look pale."

NAN LEFT her boss's office and snagged her purse and notebook. She was excited about this finding—they all suspected Eliso was being set up, but this young woman might have some information on who might be behind it—and why. That was the one thing no one could figure out—why the hell frame Eliso of all people? He was an actor—rich, yes, but not obscenely, and he had no enemies in the profession or outside of it that they knew of.

As she walked to the subway, Nan tried to think around this problem. Who had most to gain out of Eliso being in jail? His sister, Fenella, was even wealthier than he was, and from what Nan had seen of her, she adored her brother. Beulah, too, had her own money and was plainly head over heels about her lover. Stone... ha, no way. Nan had no problem in ruling him out. She allowed herself a little fantasy of Stone finding the real killer and unleashing all that machismo and rage on him. She brought herself up sharply. *Really? Violence turning you on?* She shook her head. No, it wasn't the violence, it was the thought of Stone's physicality. Over the last week, they had met three times, always at his place, mostly during her lunch break. The sex was out of this world, but Nan felt as if she was dicing with danger. Stone Vanderberg wanted her, and she knew he wouldn't wait too long before insisting she make a decision.

But... her first priority was always Ettie. Every day, every moment she spent with her daughter, she discovered new ways to love her. Ettie, with her dusky skin and her father's navy-blue eyes, was so much like Nan and her Aunt Etta—independent, warm, and loving. The innocence in her daughter's eyes, the trust, made Nan's heart ache, and she knew she would never let anyone hurt Ettie—and especially not Stone. He had been clear—he didn't want kids—and it had been the worst day of Nan's life when she saw the second blue line appear on a pregnancy test three weeks after leaving him in Antibes. Eight months later, however, she counted Ettie's birth day as the best, most magical day in her life, despite the fact she had nearly died from blood loss after Ettie's difficult birth. Waking up hours after the birth, sore, light-headed and in terrible pain, Nan had brushed all that aside as her daughter was laid against her bare breast and she began to feed her. Nan knew then... no one, no matter who, would *ever* come between them.

So, the thought of Stone rejecting Ettie made Nan's heart twist. She was being reckless, continuing to sleep with him, because she knew it could never last. But when he touched her, kissed her, she was lost.

Nan sighed and hopped onto the subway train just before the doors closed. No matter what she felt for Stone, now was not the time to think about him. She had a job to do and a witness to interview. She snagged the notebook from her purse and began to write down questions.

NAN WAS SO ABSORBED in her thoughts that she didn't notice the man at the other end of the subway carriage watching her. He felt no shame in blatantly staring at the young woman—she was gorgeous after all, and a couple of other guys nearby were also checking her out—but he assumed *they* weren't thinking of ways to kill her.

The fact she was fucking Stone might prove useful. He grinned to himself. He'd decided to follow the Songbird woman—and boy, had he hit pay dirt when he'd followed her back to her home in Oyster Bay. She had a kid—a young kid, too. A single mother was perfect—she was vulnerable in so many ways. Take the kid—she would do anything he asked. *Anything*. He wondered who the father was and if he was around. He'd found the birth certificate—no father named on it. *Huh*. Well, that was a shame.

Because when he murdered Nan Songbird, her kid was going to need to know who her father was.

At Times Square, Nan Songbird got up, and he followed her, standing too close behind her as she waited for the doors to open. He saw her glance of annoyance at the invasion of privacy, and a thrill ran through him.

Turn to face me, beautiful, open those perfect lips to tell me to back off, and I'll take this knife in my pocket and run you through with it, feel your hot blood pumping over my hands as my knife slices through your soft belly. Do it. Turn around. Give me a reason to kill you...

But she didn't, and as the doors opened, she darted into the crowds moving towards the exit. He went after her, of course, but kept his distance. What he'd just done was reckless, but hopefully she would just pass it off as another creep on the subway. He had a job to do.

He could dream about killing her later.

CHAPTER ELEVEN

Nan saw the girl sitting in the diner they had arranged to meet at and felt relief that she'd kept their appointment. "Hey, Ruthie."

The girl, goth makeup and limp black hair in need of a wash, looked up. "Hey, you the lawyer?"

Obviously, Nan thought, but smiled at her anyway. "Can I get you a drink?"

Ruthie's eyes lit up. "A JD and Coke?" She said, hopefully.

Ha. "Not a chance, kiddo, but I'll spring for a milkshake and some fries."

The light went out in Ruthie's eyes and she sighed, nodding. "Fine." Ruthie was about eighteen, Nan guessed, or maybe younger, but she had the world-weary view of someone older. 'Emo' the kids called it, but Nan guessed that in Ruthie's case, some of it was justified.

"So, tell me, did you know Willa Green?"

Ruthie shook her head. "No, like I said, I just went to see that actor because my friend offered to take me along. She had tickets—her dad is loaded—but she was shy and needed a wing man. Wing *woman*. And I thought Eliso Patini was cute, and he was—and nice, too. Friendly, down to earth."

"So, when you met him?" Nan prompted her, sipping her own tea.

"We were let into this pretty swanky conference room at the Four Seasons. There was about fifteen of us. Me and this Willa girl stood out, you know, in a room full of other girls made up perfectly and in designer gear. I thought she might be a goth, too, but when I smiled at her, she looked at me like..." She demonstrated to Nan a blank, glassy-eyed look, and Nan nodded.

"Okay, so she was a little off before Eliso got there?"

"Yup, and here's the weird thing, when he arrived, most of the girls were screaming and crying, but she looked at him like..." Ruthie trailed off and shook her head, and Nan could have screamed in frustration.

"Like she hated him?" Careful, now. No leading the witness.

Ruthie shook her head. "No, it was more like... she didn't recognize him. At *all*. She looked at all the screaming and focused on one of the hotel's staffers, expecting it to be him they were screaming at. It was like it took her a beat to focus on Eliso."

Nan took all of this in. "So, in your opinion, she didn't know who Eliso Patini was?"

"Not at all. So, when she started to scream at him, it shocked me the most, I think."

"Can you remember exactly what she said?"

Ruthie nodded, her eyes somber. "I'll never forget it. She asked him if he knew what he'd *done* to her, and when Eliso tried to calm her down, asking her calmly what was wrong, she ran over and attacked him, scratching up his face. His protection dragged her away, but Eliso ordered them not to be so rough. He was so kind. And all she could do was scream at him. 'Look what you made me do. Look what you made me do.' Then she started to cry, real wrenching sobs. Eliso tried to talk to her, but all she said was that 'he was going to get his.'" She shuddered, remembering. "She was like that kid spewing the green stuff over the priest."

Nan blinked. "Huh?"

"The Exorcist." Ruthie gave her a little smile which quickly faded. "But, seriously. It was scary. That girl was sent there by someone to say those things—I know it. Eliso Patini is no killer."

Nan decided to walk back to the office rather than take the subway again. That creep earlier had annoyed her, and she couldn't be distracted by that now. She was lost in her thoughts when her cell phone rang. Stone. "Hey, beautiful, where are you?"

"Sixth Avenue," she said, with a smile in her voice. "Although Alan gave me the afternoon off, so I actually have no idea where I'm heading. I think I just had a break in Eliso's case."

"Really?"

"Really."

"Man, that's good to hear. Listen, let me come pick you up, and we can talk about it."

Nan hesitated for a second before she agreed. "Okay, but I have to be back in Oyster Bay pretty soon." She felt her face redden even though he couldn't see her. "Just some commitments this evening."

"I'll drive you back."

Twenty minutes later, she was in the passenger seat of his Lotus. Stone smiled over at her and took her hand. "Do you have time to come back to my apartment, or shall we hang out at yours for a change?"

Nan struggled to hide a surge of panic. "Honestly, my place is a mess, floors covered in papers and other lawyer crap." *Like, what, magic wands and unicorns? Lawyer crap? Jesus, woman, get better at excuses.* "I'd be ashamed to let you see it."

"Fair enough." Stone shrugged, and Nan was relieved he didn't press the matter.

"Let's go to your place," she said, dropping her voice low, and moving her hand to cover the bulge in his jeans. She squeezed gently, and Stone groaned, his cock responding to her touch.

"God, woman, the thoughts you make me have..."

"Show me."

He swung the car into the underground garage under his building, screeched into his parking space and practically dragged her out of the car and into the elevator. His hands were underneath her skirt, ripping her panties from her one swift movement, and pushing her skirt up over her hips. Stone sank to his knees and buried his face in her groin, his tongue seeking out her clit as Nan gasped and closed her eyes. His tongue teased and swept up and down her slit, dipping deep into her cunt, making sharp stabbing movements which made her moan and beg him to never stop. He bit down on her clit, making her squeal, then standing, he unzipped his jeans and pulled out his huge cock, rock-hard and trembling.

"Open your legs further," he ordered, pinning her hands against the wall of the elevator. Nan obeyed, drawing in a sharp breath as he thrust his cock into her, fucking her hard, mercilessly as the elevator rose to his floor. If it stopped before his floor, there was no way he would be able to disconnect in time, but Nan didn't care. Stone was a master, his mouth rough on hers, his wanton desire for her thrilling and erotic.

"I could fuck you all day and all night," he growled, "and I still wouldn't be able to get enough of you, Nan Songbird."

He released her hands and lifted her into his arms, wrapping her legs around him as the door opened directly to his penthouse, and he carried her into his apartment. They tumbled to the floor, and Stone was immediately inside her again, kicking her legs wide apart in a way that sent delight and a thrill racing through her, thrusting deep inside her, filling her. Her cunt constricted around his cock, and she tightened her thighs around him, enhancing the friction between them until they were both coming, uninhibited and unrestrained, clawing at each other.

Stone bit down on her shoulder, and she dug her fingernails into his back hard enough to leave marks. They play-fought, not caring if they drew blood, fucking themselves senseless until both were exhausted and panting for air. They lay, naked, on his plush carpet, gazing at each other and laughing. Stone rolled onto his side. "Have I told you that your body is perfect?" He drew a hand down her side and cupped a breast.

Nan smiled. "I could do with losing about ten pounds, but thank you."

"Don't you dare lose an ounce," he said, but smiled. "Seriously, the curves of you... lie back for me, beautiful, and I'm going to show you just how perfect you are."

Nan did as he asked, and she was surprised she felt no embarrassment at his compliments. Stone caressed her feet in his hands. "Tiny little feet," he said, then slid his hands up to cradle her calves. "Silky skin." His fingers drifted to her inner thighs, parting her legs a little. His fingertips stroked the soft flesh of her thigh while his lips found her clit again.

He smiled up at her. "My heaven." Nan smiled down at him.

"Rude boy."

He chuckled as he trailed his lips up her belly. "I swear to

God, your belly is the most erotic part for me—your deep, round bellybutton..." He dipped his tongue into it, mimicking his cock as he orally fucked her navel, rimming it, kissing it. Nan writhed in pleasure, moaning softly.

Stone grinned wickedly. "You like that don't you? Well, my tongue is going upwards, but if you like..." He swapped his tongue for his thumb, pressing it hard into her navel as his lips moved up the line from her stomach, then fixed around each of her nipples in turn. "Sweet, ripe breasts, pillowy and soft, and your nipples... little buds, so sweet..."

Nan was lost in a world of pleasure, but she still felt a pang. They were sweet with milk for *their* child... the child Stone didn't know exist. She wanted to tell him at that moment, but then he was kissing her mouth and thrusting his cock back inside her and she lost the nerve.

They fucked for hours until the light outside the window started fading and Nan checked her watch. "I really have to go."

She and Stone dressed, and then he offered her his hand. "Come on."

As they drove out to Oyster Bay, Nan argued with herself. She had sent Carrie a text message telling her that she would pick up Ettie later, but now she faced a quandary.

She knew she was falling for Stone, and that she meant she was falling *in love*, but there was no way it could go any further without her telling him about Ettie. It would break her heart now if he rejected them both, but she couldn't imagine the pain down the line if the same thing happened.

And besides, it wasn't fair to him to keep him in the dark. No... it was time.

As THEY PULLED up to her house, Stone reached over to kiss her. "Now, you can either invite me in, or I can go. Which is it?"

Nan hesitated then, as she was about to invite him in, let him see the nursery, and tell him the truth, but after a glance in the rear-view mirror, her nerve failed. She saw Carrie, a harried look on her face, pushing Ettie's pram up the hill to Nan's house. Shit, she was out of time.

"Stone..."

His cell phone rang, and he glanced at it, annoyed at the interruption. His face cleared. "Hey, sorry, I have to get this. Ted? Everything okay?"

Nan swallowed, her face flaming red as she watched Carrie approach. Thank God Stone's windows were tinted. She looked at her lover and was shocked to see the expression on his face.

"Yes. Yes, I understand," he was saying. His usually stoic face was creased with grief. "Look, I'm on the island... I can be there in ten minutes. Okay, okay, see you then."

He ended the call and rubbed his face.

"Are you okay?" Nan touched his cheek, and he held her hand to his face, his eyes closed as he shook his head.

"No. No, I'm not... my father just died. I have to go."

NAN SAID goodbye and got out of the car, telling Stone to call if he needed anything. *God, poor Stone.* The feelings she had felt at her own parent's passing came flooding back. No matter what age you were, you never got over it.

Carrie caught up to her. "Oh, thank God, Nan. I'm so sorry, but Jed's sick and I have to get back to him."

Nan took Ettie, sound asleep, and hugged Carrie with one arm. "I'm so sorry."

"Look, I might need to quarantine him if it's serious, so..."

Nan's heart sank, but she smiled at Carrie. "It's no problem, Carrie, I can work from home for a few days. You go above and beyond for me. If there's anything I can do..."

. . .

AFTER CARRIE LEFT, Nan took Ettie into the house and locked the door behind her. So much trauma. She sat down on the couch with Ettie nestled in her arms and snuggled up to her, breathing in her powdery scent. "I love you so much, Tee-Tee," she whispered to her daughter. Ettie, in her sleep, splayed out her tiny fingers and pushed them against Nan's cheek.

"Bug, bug, sleepy bug," Nan crooned softly and closed her eyes, pressing her lips to her daughter's tiny forehead. She thought about Stone, racing to be with his family at their massive compound on the other side of the community. She realized with a jolt of guilt and grief that Ettie's grandfather had just died. The grandfather who didn't know she existed. *Oh God...*

Tears began to pour down her cheeks and for the first time, Nan knew what a huge mistake she had made. "What have I done, Tee-Tee?" Tears dropped from her eyes as she began to cry quietly.

What have I done?

CHAPTER TWELVE

Stone's heart felt like it was beating slower today. As he carried his father's casket up the long aisle of the cathedral, he didn't feel the weight of it, just a heavy rock of grief which had settled in his chest.

He saw Eliso and Beulah holding hands, both looking as sorrowful as he did. Eliso touched his arm as he passed, a silent promise of support. Stone's mother Diana was weeping quietly at the front of the congregation, supported by Stone's aunt and uncle. His brother, Ted, also one of his father's pallbearers nodded to him as they set the casket down on the plinth at the front and returned to their mother's side.

Stone looked around, searching the congregation. A weight lifted when he saw her, hovering in the back row. *Nan.* She had come. He wanted to go to her now, hold her hand and have her wrap her arms around him, comfort him. She was the first person he had thought of this morning, and it had shaken him to his core. He, Stone Vanderberg, *needed* her. She felt like home to him now. In the few days since his father's death, they had talked more than they ever had. And ironically, they hadn't seen each other since that day. Nan had told him he needed to be with his family, but if he needed her, she could meet him back in Oyster Bay.

In the end, his mother had taken up all of his time, and he hadn't managed to get away, but they had spoken every night until they were too tired to speak anymore. One morning, Stone had woken to find he hadn't hung up the phone, and he listened to her sleep for a few moments before ending the call. He didn't want her to think he was some sort of creeper, but he wanted to know what it would be like to wake up with her. Yes, they had done so in France, but now, when their relationship seemed so different... he wanted more. He wanted her all the time —forever.

She met his gaze now and gave him a sweet smile, mouthing, "Are you okay?"

I adore you. It was on the tip of his tongue to mouth it back at her, but this wasn't the time or place. He nodded instead and mouthed, "Thank you for coming."

Nan put her hand over her heart and Stone felt rare tears prick his eyes. No, he wasn't going to cry now. He'd held back for days now, not even letting himself break in private. But at that moment he acknowledged to himself the basic truth: he was in love with Nan Songbird.

AT THE WAKE, he had to do his duty and commiserate with his extended family before he finally could seek out Nan. She was with Eliso and Beulah who were obviously steering her through the inquisitive family members. Some of them had obviously caught the connection between him and Nan, so he didn't hesitate in kissing her mouth when he finally caught up with them. "Thanks for coming," he murmured against her lips, "it means the world."

Nan hugged him tightly, then released him, but she slipped her hand into his. "How are you?"

"Not great, but better now you're here. Hey Eli, Beulah, thank you for coming."

"Of course, brother." Eliso embraced his friend, and Beulah kissed Stone's cheek. "Is there anything we can do for you?"

"You're doing it by just being here, all of you." He squeezed Nan's hand. "Can I talk to you outside for a moment?"

Outside, the weather was turning cooler as fall approached. Nan shivered, and Stone wrapped his arms around her. "I mean it, you being here makes this all bearable."

Nan kissed him. "I'm so sorry about your dad, Stone. I really am."

"I don't get it... he was physically fit and only in his mid-sixties."

"How did it happen?"

"Mom said he got sick after a meal out with Ted. The coroner said he might have had an allergic reaction to something he ate, but we didn't know of any allergies. Toxicology will take a while to come back. Shit. Mom's... devastated. She lost her best friend, her partner in life, her love." Stone closed his eyes and leaned his forehead against Nan's. "I could say that I don't know how that feels... but it wouldn't be true. Not anymore. I don't want the first time I say *I love you* to be at my father's funeral... but just know. You are my life now, Nan Songbird."

There were tears in her eyes, and Nan looked as if she was about to say something to him when from behind they heard a voice. "Hey."

Turning, Stone saw his brother looking at them, his eyes hooded and watchful. Ted smiled a humorless smile at them both. "Are you going to introduce me to your friend, Stone?"

"Of course." Tension crept into Stone's demeanor—Ted was drunk. Stone could see it in his eyes. He loved his brother with all his heart, but he knew how many demands he had, too, and he was wary of the looks Ted was giving Nan. "Nanouk Songbird, this is my brother, Edward Vanderberg... Ted to us. Ted, this is my... girlfriend, Nan."

Nan shook Ted's hand, but from her quiet manner, she, too, had noticed the malice in his brother's eyes. She looked at Stone for reassurance as Ted sipped more whiskey from his glass.

"How long has this been going on?"

Stone put his arm around Nan's shoulders. "For a while. Over a year... kind of." He smiled down at Nan, who gave him a weak smile he didn't quite understand. "We met last year at the Cannes Film Festival, Ted. Nan is a lawyer. Actually she's Eliso's defense lawyer."

"And how did you meet?" Ted's tone was condescending and Stone frowned at him. What was his problem?

Before he could say anything, Nan spoke up. From the tone of her voice, she wasn't impressed with Stone's brother. "Stone saved me from being raped and murdered by a man called Duggan Smollett. After that, we got to know each other."

"Got to... *know*... each other?"

"That's enough, Ted." Stone had reached his limit. He grabbed Ted's upper arm and steered him towards the house. "Go inside and get some coffee into you. You're an embarrassment, and Mom doesn't need that today."

Ted's smile faded, and he suddenly looked like a lost little boy. "Yeah. Sorry." He looked back at Nan with a small smile. "I'm sorry. It was good to meet you."

"You, too," said Nan. Stone appreciated the lie. Today wasn't the day for unpleasantness.

LATER, Nan came to find him to say goodbye. "I wish you would stay," he said regretfully, but she shook her head.

"Thank you but you need to be with your family right now."

Stone stroked her hair back from her face. "Will we ever wake up together again? I miss that."

Nan nodded. "I do, too... it's just complicated at the moment."

"Let's uncomplicate it. Move in with me."

Nan drew in a deep breath. "I can't...not yet, Stone."

Stone kissed her. "Just think about it, is all I ask."

"I promise." She kissed him goodbye and went back out to her car. Her battered old Honda looked incongruous next to the Bentleys, Lotuses, and Mercedes on the long gravel driveway.

As she drove to the rail station, her emotions were in a turmoil. Nan knew she had made a mistake by not telling Stone about Ettie from the start, because now the word *love* was being bandied around, and she couldn't help but feel panicked about it.

She caught the train back into the city and to the office. Alan met her at the door. "I have bad news."

"God, what?"

"Ruthie's missing. We went to pick her up to take her to the safe house before her testimony, and the police were there."

Nan felt sick. "What did they find?"

"Blood. A lot of it."

"Oh, God, no..." Nan sank into a chair, covering her face with her hands. Alan patted her shoulder.

"I hate to say this, but at least we got her to talk to the police before this. We can still use this to try to get the charges against Eliso dismissed."

"But what about Ruthie?"

"The police have got this, Nan. I am sorry, but it's out of our hands now. Look, I've filed a motion to dismiss; I doubt just Ruthie's statement will be enough, but you never know."

"Okay." Nan rubbed her forehead. Poor Ruthie. "Look, I need

to know why the DA is pursuing this, especially when witnesses are being... attacked." She still held out hope that Ruthie was alive somewhere. "This is getting dangerous."

"I know. Be careful out there, Nan. We have no idea who is behind all of this."

ALAN'S WARNING made her feel paranoid as she caught the train back to Oyster Bay that evening. When she picked Ettie up from Carrie's place, her eyes darted around her as she walked quickly back to their home, and she double-locked everything before she could relax. Ettie was fast asleep, her little cheeks moving as she pulled on her pacifier. Nan felt exhausted, her body heavy, her breasts heavy with milk. She laid Ettie in her crib, then snuck the breast pump out of the nursery and closed the door slightly.

She made herself some tea then sat on the couch, head back, expressing her milk. "This is so sexy," she said to herself, and chuckled. What they *don't* tell you about feeding your baby...

Despite the tug on her nipples, she felt herself relaxing, drifting off to sleep. Why the hell was she so tired lately? Was it the marathon sex with Stone? Or working all hours on Eliso's case? As she fell asleep, her last waking thought was her sorrow at Ruthie's abduction...

A LOUD KNOCKING WOKE her up and dazed, she clambered to answer the door before the caller's knocking woke Ettie. She wasn't even thinking straight when she yanked open the door and jumped back with a shock.

Stone grinned at her and opened his mouth to speak, just as Ettie woke up and began to cry.

CHAPTER THIRTEEN

A myriad of emotions went through Stone's body, but the most vivid of them was confusion. Nan, her blouse obviously pushed together hastily, was looking at him with guilt written all over her face. When the baby started to cry, she looked panicked.

"*Complicated.*" Stone repeated back to her. He got it now. She had someone else at home—*that* was why she never let him come here. And not only that... they had a *child.*

Stone's heart froze at that moment. "I can see I'm interrupting. I'll go." Everything in his body urged him to push past her and beat the living crap of the man was inside.

Nan stared at him and for a second, he thought she was going to beg him to stay. But then she closed her eyes and shook her head. "No."

Stone turned on his heel. "You'll have to do better than that, Nanouk. This is more than a... *Jesus*... this goes beyond lying."

"You're right. Stone, please. Come inside and I'll explain."

He hesitated, but his curiosity won over his hurt, and he nodded curtly. "Just the truth."

"I swear to God."

He followed her inside, expecting to see a man. Instead she walked to the back of the cottage into another room. Stone waited in the living room. Soon Nan emerged, carrying a young child—a very young child—in her arms. His heart began to beat faster.

"Stone... this is Ettie. She was born four months ago." Nan's voice was quivering, but Stone couldn't take his eyes off the child. She had Nan's caramel-colored skin and dark hair... but her navy-blue eyes were unmistakable.

Stone looked at Nan. He needed to hear her confirm it. She nodded. "Yes. Yes, Ettie is your daughter, Stone."

Stone stared at her in horror as she began to cry softly.

HOURS LATER. *Hours.* Nan's heart had been wrung out, frozen, and shattered. She lay on her bed with Ettie asleep next to her. So, this was it then—it was just her and Ettie against the world now. She'd risked her heart with Stone—and lost.

He didn't want them.

Even now, as she said it to herself, she couldn't believe it. He'd opened his mouth to speak, then as she held out his daughter to him, he'd turned and walked out of the house, closing the door quietly after him. She wondered why he hadn't slammed it, but she was grateful for that one last consideration.

God, you fool, Songbird. You almost had it all, and because you were a coward, you blew it.

Nan pressed her lips to Ettie's plump cheek. "We just have each other now," she whispered and drew in a deep breath. "And that's okay."

That's okay. She said it to herself again and again until she fell into a fitful sleep, awakened after only a couple of hours by Alan calling to tell her that the charges against Eliso had been dropped.

. . .

Eliso asked Alan to say everything twice before he believed it. "It's over?"

"The *charges* are over. Miles Kirke called to tell me himself. What bugs me is that he didn't sound upset in the least. He lost and he's cheerful about it? I don't like this—he's up to something."

Nan frowned. "Did he say why?"

"He says Ruthie's testimony struck a chord."

"Bullshit," Nan stopped herself, "Sorry. I don't buy it."

Beulah nodded. "I agree. None of this has ever made sense, so why now? And for one witness' testimony? Yeah, I'm with Nan. This stinks."

"It does, but for now let's be grateful that the charges were dropped. Your passport will be returned to you, Eliso, but don't leave New York right away—just in case."

"Fine. Beulah has a shoot coming up in Manhattan, and I'm not due to be on my next movie set for a month."

"Good. Keep in touch and I'll do the same."

When Alan had gone back to his office, Nan sat with Eliso and Beulah for a time. "How do you feel?" Nan asked Eliso.

"Weirded out. This morning I was facing murder charges and now? None of this seems real."

"I would keep your wits about you. Someone wanted to set you up, Eliso, and that person is still out there."

"I know."

Beulah was studying Nan, and Nan wondered if Stone had told her. "You look tired, Nan. Why don't you have dinner with us?"

Nan smiled at her. "Can I take a raincheck? Don't tell Alan, but I'm going to go see Miles Kirke and ask him what his game is."

"Is that safe?"

"Kirke's too wily to get involved with anything dangerous. I'm willing to bet he thought this was going to go one way and didn't think we'd find anything to prove you were being set up. He's doing damage control now, and I think I can get him on our side."

"Girl power." Beulah grinned at her and Nan chuckled.

"Something like that."

MILES KIRKE IS A SMUG, *self-centered narcissist*, Nan decided an hour later as he smirked at her from across his vast antique desk. Or rather *made* to look antique, she realized. The desk was like Kirke himself—outwardly impressive and expansive—inward shallow and cheap.

"I don't know what to tell you, Ms. Songbird, other than you convinced me. Eliso Patini is no more a killer than I am."

Nan's eyes narrowed. *Condescending prick.* "Forgive me for speaking my mind, Mr. Kirke, but this whole thing has been flimsy from the start, and I can't help thinking it was just a publicity stunt."

Something like anger flickered in the man's eyes, and Nan knew her barb had hit home. "Ms. Songbird... does your boss know you are here making these accusations?"

"No, and I am not making accusations, Mr. Kirke, merely asking why the profound lack of evidence brought both charges and *dropped* charges?"

Miles Kirke sat up and tee-peed his fingers in front of him. "You know, sometimes that's just the way life works out. Listen, Ms. Songbird, I've been watching you, observing your career. You have a lot of tenacity, something that could be utilized to great effect in this office."

"Are you offering me a job as a way of distracting me, Mr. Kirke?" God, the man was obsequious.

"No, I'm offering you a job as a way of poaching you from Elizondo. You and I would make a great team."

Ugh, really? The way his eyes roamed over her body told her *exactly* what kind of team he was talking about. "Well, you've very kind, but I am happy where I am, thank you."

"And Stone Vanderberg? Is he happy the way things are?"

Nan went very still. "Excuse me?"

Miles smirked again, and she wanted to punch it off his face. "People talk. I listen."

"I suggest you expunge any gossip you may or may not have heard about my private life, Mr. Kirke." She stood up. "Thank you for your time."

"I bet you are a spectacular fuck."

Nan whirled around. "What the hell did you just say to me?"

Kirke, too, had risen from his chair, and he darted around the desk and grabbed her wrists. "You heard me. What about it, Nan? Let me sample the wares. I hear Vanderberg is crazy about you, and he's not one easily won over."

Nan kneed him in the balls, and he crumpled, but still choked out a laugh.

"You despicable scumbag," Nan said, wild with anger. "Your boss will hear about this."

"Oh, I don't think so," Miles said, recovering quickly and shooting her a nasty grin. He limped to his desk and pulled out a manila folder from his desk and threw it at her. "I don't think either you or Stone Vanderberg would want your daughter's name in the press anytime soon. Patini's lawyer fucking the best friend way ahead of time? Sounds like conflict of interest to me."

Nan gaped at him. "You had me *followed*?"

"Of course. I always do my due diligence on my opposition. You met Vanderberg in Cannes last year, had an affair, and gave birth to his daughter before reconnecting with him this year. Get that baby-daddy money, huh, Songbird?"

Nan felt like she could both throw up and cry. She grabbed her purse and slammed out of Kirke's office, catching sight of his secretary's sympathetic glance. Clearly this kind of assault was par for the curse. *Asshole.*

Nan knew one thing as she took the train home that night. She'd had just about enough of men lately. She picked up Ettie, holding her daughter close, letting the scent of her, her warmth be a balm to her frazzled nerves. God forbid Ettie should ever have to put up with this kind of harassment and sexual assault. Both Duggan Smollett and Miles Kirke were of the same kind—entitled rich men who took what they wanted. If she could, she would bring them both down.

As she slid her key into the lock on her door, she heard her name being called and turned. A young, pleasant-faced man was calling to her. "Miss Songbird? Miss Nanouk Songbird?"

"That's me."

He handed her an envelope. "Congrats, you've been served. Have a good day."

What the hell? She watched him as he sauntered back to his car and gave her a cheery wave. Make that *three* men on her shit list. She carried Ettie inside and fed and bathed her before she opened the letter. Ettie was gurgling happily on her play mat when Nan finally had the headspace to take in the contents. It was from an Upper East Side lawyer even more exclusive than Alan. She read through the contents of the letter and gave a gasp of utter horror.

Stone was suing her for custody of Ettie.

14

CHAPTER FOURTEEN

Eliso and Beulah walked back to their hotel through town, only being stopped occasionally by fans. Eliso posed for selfies and signed autographs with a smile and a kind word, but he was glad to get back to the sanctuary of their hotel suite. Beulah kissed his eyelids.

"Everyone's so tired," she remarked. "Nan didn't look well, did she?"

"I really don't know her enough to say either way," Eliso said, "but I think we're all drained."

Beulah tangled her fingers in his dark curls. "I know the perfect way to celebrate your freedom."

Eliso smiled. "And how is that?"

Beulah grinned and went into the bathroom. "A shared hot soak in the tub, a good meal…"

"And?"

He heard her chuckle from inside the bathroom. "And lots and lots of dirty sex."

"Now you're talking." Eliso pulled his tie off and slipped his jacket off. Beulah came back into the room. "Starting without me?"

"Never."

"Then let me do that."

Eliso shook his head. "Oh no. Tonight, I'm the one in charge, *Bella*."

Beulah grinned as he took her hands and turned them over, pressing his lips to the inside of each of her wrists. "I do love you, my scruffy Italian."

"*Ti amo, Bella* Beulah, *ti amo...*"

He slid his hands under her dress and pulled it over her head. Her breasts, perky and full, needed no bra, and he bent his head to take her nipple into his mouth as she stroked his dark curls. His fingertips stroked her belly, softly curved and quivering under his touch, then moved down to draw her panties down her long legs.

"You are a goddess," he whispered, his lips against her belly and she chuckled, then gasped as he pushed her legs apart and took her clit into his mouth.

He heard her moan and smiled, his hands clamping onto her perfect ass as he went down on her. "God, Eli... I want your cock..."

He persisted until she came, then stood, stripping his jeans and underwear off as Beulah tore his shirt from him. His cock was throbbing, almost painfully hard as he swept her into his arms and carried her to bed.

"I want to suck you first," Beulah said to him, and he nodded as she took him into her warm mouth. The sight of his cock moving in and out of her beautiful lips made him even harder, and he came on her tongue as she drank him down. He was already stiffening again in anticipation as he pushed her back onto the bed, and she spread her legs wide, giving him a beautiful view of her red, swollen cunt, so wet and ready for him.

"*Mio Dio*, Beulah, *mio Dio...*" He covered her body with his and pressed his engorged cock deep inside her as she writhed beneath him, reaming her hard, feeling her fingers digging into his flesh, urging him deeper, harder, longer.

They fucked for hours, laughing and joking around between couplings, both relieved that the nightmare was over. Beulah rested her head on his chest. "Who would want to set you up like this?"

"Well, that's the question, isn't it? Has been all along. I just wish... well, that they'd come after me and not dragged that poor girl into this. If someone wanted to hurt me, why not come after me?"

"Or me."

Eliso shivered. "Don't ever say that, Bella. Besides, with our security, no one would get near you."

Beulah raised her head to look him in the eye. "Eli?"

"Yes, Bebé?"

She smiled, and he marveled over her soft, exotic beauty. "Will you marry me?"

Eliso grinned. "Stealing all my lines. Be patient, girl. I'm going to ask very soon."

"I'm not being impatient. Like I said to Nan, girl power. Will you, Eliso Dario Patini, do me the honor of becoming my husband?"

Eliso sat up and pulled her to him, kissing her hard. "Beulah Tegan, nothing, and I mean, *nothing* would give me greater pleasure than to be your husband. Yes. *Yes, of course.*"

Beulah squealed and gave him a million kisses all over his face as he laughed. "We should get champagne." She glanced over at the clock. Three A.M. "You think they'll let us have some?"

Eliso rolled his eyes. "I'm sure it'll be no problem, babe." He hooked the phone up and called room service. Grinning at her, he spoke to the night manager. "Yes, please. Your two most expensive bottles. Sorry? Oh, yes, yes, that would be excellent. We're celebrating. Thank you."

He hung up and kissed Beulah on the mouth. "Your champagne is on its way, Bella. We're going to drink one bottle. The other I'm going to spray all over your sensational body and lick every drop off slowly."

Beulah moaned in anticipation and straddled him. "And while we're waiting…"

She guided his cock into her and they made love slowly, Eliso running his hands over her breasts, her belly, pulling her down on top of him so he could kiss her mouth. "*Ti amo*," he murmured, his lips against hers and knew it to be his truth. This woman in his arms… no one could ever come close. They fit each other so perfectly.

They made each other come just seconds before the champagne arrived, brought by the night manager himself—Eliso was a superstar after all. Their treatment at the hotel had become an awful lot better now that the charges had been dropped.

"I come with an apology, Sir. Our ice machine is out of service, but I'm happy to fill the bucket from the ice station down the corridor."

Eliso waved him off, slipping a generous tip into his hand. "No, it's okay. I got this. Thank you, we appreciate the trouble you've gone to."

The night manager, a sleekly handsome Englishman, smiled at them both. "And may I express my and the hotel's congratulations to you both?"

"Thank you." Beulah gave him a sweet smile, and Eliso shook the man's hand.

When they were alone, Eliso grabbed the ice bucket. "Back in a moment."

Beulah waved her phone at him. "Take your time. I'm calling London."

"Can't wait to tell your mom?" Eliso smiled at her, and she grinned.

"She's so in love with you I'll just be making her jealous."

"Haha."

Beulah smiled. "Honey, I don't know how to tell you this, but..." She nodded to his groin, and he realized with a groan that his zipper was undone. "No wonder the night manager was smiling." Beulah stuck her tongue in her cheek, then giggled.

In the corridor, Eliso filled both ice buckets, and as he was balancing them for the trip back, an elderly woman wandered up and squinted at him. "Oh, goodie. I won!"

Eliso blinked. "I'm sorry?"

"You're that handsome Italian man, the actor... Shirley?!" She bellowed down the quiet hall, and Eliso hid a grin. Another elderly woman stuck her head out of a room up ahead. "Wendy, keep your voice down." She, too, peered at Eliso, and Wendy looked triumphant,

"You owe me fifty bucks! It *is* him!"

"Good grief." Shirley came out of the room and tottered down the hall toward them. When she reached them, she put up her hand and touched Eliso's face. "Goodness, you're a beautiful boy. You're right, Wendy, it *is* him."

"And you owe me fifty bucks."

Shirley waved her hand. "Yes, yes." She pulled out an iPhone from her pocket. "Can we have a selfie, dear?"

Eliso grinned at them. "Of course, it would be my pleasure." Both Wendy and Shirley snuggled in close as they took the picture. Beulah, still on her phone, poked her head out of the room and saw them. She grinned.

"Is that your girlfriend?" Shirley said, enviously, and Eliso chuckled.

"That's my fiancée," he said, proudly. Beulah blew them a kiss and disappeared back into their room. Shirley and Wendy weren't about to let their prize escape just yet and peppered him with questions. Kind hearted as always, Eliso chatted to them and was about to offer to take them both to lunch with himself and Beulah the next day when a terrified, wrenching scream tore through the quiet hallways.

Eliso dropped the ice buckets and ran towards the screams—he knew instantly that it was his love, his Beulah, who needed his help.

He dashed into the room—and saw her. Beulah was on the floor. Blood everywhere. She looked up at him with terrified eyes, then her gaze shifted to something behind him. "No, don't hurt him, *no*..."

Eliso began to turn—and everything went dark.

As ELISO FELL unconscious to the floor, Beulah gasped in agony as her attacker returned to her. "Please... don't..."

She couldn't see anything but his eyes, devoid of any empathy or mercy. She'd just said goodbye to her mom when he had grabbed her from behind and stabbed her in the small of her back. Beulah had screamed, and he'd thrown her to the floor just as Eliso had arrived. Grabbing a heavy statue from the hotel desk, he'd slammed it into Eliso's head as she screamed.

Now, he tugged her robe apart as she tried to fight him. "Why?" Beulah pleaded with him as he drew back his arm. "Why are you doing this?"

He stopped suddenly and bent down and whispered something in her ear, and Beulah gasped. As her eyes widened with a shock of revelation and fear, her attacker plunged his knife into her belly again and again until Beulah could no longer breathe.

Her last living thought was of the man she loved... *Eliso... Eliso... I love you... I love you so much...*

HER KILLER WITHDREW his knife and wiped her blood on her robe. His groin was taut, rock-hard as he studied his handiwork. Such a beautiful girl. He closed her eyes and traced the outline of her lips. He had whispered to her, told her he was killing her because she was beautiful, because she loved Eliso, and because he would enjoy it—and she'd had terror in her eyes as she died.

He heard voices and slipped quickly away, hearing cries as he ran from the hall and down the stairs. He wasn't worried about being identified; he had chosen his clothing well: all black to hide the blood, a full head balaclava to hide his features.

Outside in the dawn, he darted down an alleyway and tossed the head covering in a dumpster. Earlier he'd stashed a blazer behind it, something to put over his dark clothes to make him look less sinister as he made his escape.

He walked calmly out of the alley and to the nearest subway station. He bought a newspaper and read it like any other commuter on his way to work. As he reached his office, he greeted his personal assistant and asked her to bring him coffee.

Only when he was alone, did he allow himself to think of the murder, to relive it, revel in the cold excitement of it. Soon, it would be all over the news. Eliso's beautiful fiancée slain, Patini himself attacked and left unconscious.

He smiled to himself. He would enjoy reliving her murder and was looking forward to the next one he was determined to commit: Patini's lawyer friend. "Stone's paramour"

Nan Songbird.

15

CHAPTER FIFTEEN

Nan wanted to run through the hospital, but with a sleeping Ettie in her arms, she had to settle for a fast walk. Even though she knew Stone would be there, she had to come. She saw Alan and headed toward him, and then realized he was talking to Stone. Stone looked broken.

He stood up as he saw her. "Thank you for coming," he said softly.

"Of course, of course... is there any news?"

"Eliso is still in surgery. The blow he took was hard enough to cause a brain bleed."

Nan felt sick. "Oh God... and Beulah?"

Stone and Alan exchanged a look, and Nan knew. Beulah was dead. "Oh no... *no*..."

Her legs gave way, and Stone steered her into a chair. "Let me hold her for a moment while you collect yourself."

Nan handed Ettie to him without hesitation, something she would later marvel at. Alan sat down next to Nan. "The police found them both, and brought them here, but Beulah was dead on arrival. She had been stabbed repeatedly, like Willa Green."

"Jesus... and probably Ruthie, too." Nan closed her eyes and leaned forward, dark spots at the corners of her eyes. "Poor, poor Beulah... all that... life, that joy, just gone... I don't believe it."

She looked up at Stone, and a thrill of both warmth and fear jolted through her. He was gazing down at his daughter, and Nan was shocked to see wonder in his eyes. He met her gaze, and it disappeared. *God... he hates me.* She stood and held her hands out. "I can take her now."

Stone handed Ettie back to her without protest. "I'm going to find out what I can from the surgical staff."

He turned on his heel and stalked down the corridor. Nan sighed, hugging Ettie closer to herself. Alan was watching her carefully. "Something I should know? I thought you two were friends?"

Nan drew in a deep breath. "Alan... Ettie is Stone Vanderberg's daughter. You know we had a relationship while I was in France last year? Well, I found out I was pregnant when I got back, and you know the rest."

"Not quite. Vanderberg didn't know about Ettie?"

She could hear the judgment in her boss's voice and didn't blame him. "He told me last year, quite clearly that he never wanted to have kids. Never. So, I didn't tell him—hell, I never thought I'd see him again. Then Eliso Patini got charged with murder. God, poor Eliso..."

Alan was ruminating on what she'd told him, and she studied his expression. "You think I did the wrong thing?"

He sighed. "It's not for me to tell you how to run your life, Nan."

"He's suing me for custody."

Alan's eyebrows shot up. "What?"

"Quite."

They sat in silence for a long time. "Nan, playing devil's advocate..."

"Go on."

"He looks like a man in pain. When he held Ettie... now I'm not saying I'm a body language expert or a psychologist, but he just lost his father. Then he found out he had a child. *Then* his best friend was attacked and the fiancée brutally murdered. Maybe..." He looked at sleeping Ettie, and his face softened. "Maybe you and she are what he needs right now. He's just reacting out of pain and shock."

"You think so?"

"He's right." They both started as Stone's voice broke the quiet. He was looking at Nan, terrible pain in his eyes, and it shattered her heart. "Can we talk?"

Alan got up and patted him on the back. "No one is in the relative's room... why don't you go in there? I'll wait here for any news."

NAN DIDN'T KNOW what to think of Stone's request, but what he did was the last thing she expected. He closed the door behind them as they stepped into the cold, clinical relative's room, and then came to her and Ettie. Gently, he pressed his lips to his daughter's forehead and kissed Nan, his mouth firm against hers. He leaned his forehead against hers. "I'm sorry. I really didn't mean... it doesn't matter now. I get it now. I get why you didn't tell me—I do."

"I never meant to hurt you," she whispered, "but I had to protect Ettie."

"I know." He stroked a finger across Ettie's plump little cheek. "She's so beautiful, Nan."

Tears dropped down Nan's cheeks. "She is and so loving, Stone. Look, I know you don't want..."

"I was a fool. How could I not want her?" He looked up at Nan. "The *both* of you. You must know, Nan, that I'm in love with you—so utterly in love." He gave a small laugh. "I'm new at this,

I admit. You have me... bemused, enchanted, incredulous, Nanouk Songbird. And you, Ettie Songbird... you are the best, purest thing in this world."

Nan started to weep now, and Stone enclosed both of them in his arms. Nan looked up at him, her eyes red. "I love you, too," she said, her voice cracking. "So much... I was scared and reckless, but I don't regret loving you or having Ettie. You and she are the best things that ever happened to me, and I'm sorry I screwed things up so badly. Can you forgive me?"

"There's nothing to forgive, Nan, nothing." He stroked her face, then his eyes grew serious. "I do have one request... it's obvious now that whoever is targeting Eliso will stop at nothing to make him suffer. The killer didn't kill Eliso for a good reason—this isn't over, and I think we are all in danger. So... would you and Ettie come live with me, for the time being? My building is safe, and of course, I have a whole security team on hand."

Nan hesitated. Was this too much, too soon? She knew the danger they might be in, but living with him? She looked down at her sleeping daughter and made her decision. "Alright. Until the killer is behind bars. Then... well, we'll have to reassess if we're ready for that."

Stone's shoulders relaxed. "Good. Thank you. As for the other thing, I'll call my lawyer and ask him to drop the custody case. I would like to be recognized as Ettie's father, though, but it's your decision."

Nan gazed up at him. "We can work that out, too."

Stone bent his head and kissed her, then sighed. "God, I feel like I can't think straight with Eli in so much trouble."

"I know what you mean. I keep thinking about Beulah..." Nan's voice cracked a little. "Why would anyone kill her?"

Stone shook his head. "I can't even begin to imagine the psychopath's reasoning. The police say it looked like a thrill kill."

"He *enjoyed* it?"

Stone looked as sick as Nan felt. Alan knocked on the door. "Hey, sorry to interrupt but the surgeon is here."

ELISO PATINI WOKE, his head screaming with pain, but more than that, his heart broken into a million pieces. He knew she was gone; he felt it deep in his marrow. A doctor hovered into view. "Mr. Patini? How do you feel?"

Like I'm in hell. "Confused." He had to know, he still held onto a little hope. "Beulah?"

The doctor didn't need to say the words, but Eliso needed to hear them. "I'm so sorry, Mr. Patini, but we tried everything to save Ms. Tegan. Her injuries were too catastrophic."

Mio Dio... Eliso closed his eyes and wished he didn't ever have to open them again.

"Eli?" A sweet, familiar voice. Fenella slipped her hand into his. He opened his eyes to look at his sister. Fenella had red-rimmed eyes with dark shadows underneath. Her cheeks were wet with tears. "Eli... I'm so sorry."

"I'm glad you're here, Fen." His voice was gruff and gravelly, and his throat was parched. "I need some water."

"Ice chips only for now, I'm afraid, just while we monitor your progress." The surgeon pressed Eli's hand. "You've had major brain surgery, Mr. Patini."

Eliso nodded, then wished he hadn't. Everything hurt, but nothing more than the loss of Beulah. "I keep thinking she'll come into the room, fussing over me, cracking jokes." God, how could this be real?

Fenella nodded. "Believe it or not, so do I. I wish I had been nicer to her, but I was jealous. Jealous that she was taking my little brother away from me, as silly as that sounds now. Petty, stupid feelings that stopped me from being her friend. Eli, I will regret that forever. Beulah was a wonderful person."

"Thank you for saying that." He looked around for a clock. "How long have I been out?"

Fen swallowed. "A week. They operated on you the night you came in and then again two days later. Your brain swelled, so they had to relieve the pressure. It's a relief you can communicate so well; we were all terrified you wouldn't be *you* or even if you would wake up. They started to bring you out of the coma this morning."

A *week*. "Beulah's parents?"

"We flew them over the same day, don't worry. Beulah's mom has been sitting with you, holding your hand. So has Nan and Stone. Did you know they had a baby together?"

Eli's eyes widened. "No... *what*? Are you sure?"

"Pretty sure. Ettie. She's adorable and Stone is besotted. Never thought I'd see that happen."

"Fuck." Eliso felt a wave of sadness. How had the world changed in such a short time? Beulah was dead and Stone was a *father*? It was too much to comprehend, and he felt exhausted. He looked at his sister. "Beulah... her funeral?"

Fen looked uncomfortable. "Her parents want to take her body back to London, but they also want you to have a say in it. They hoped you would be awake before they had to make the decision. For now, Beulah is being cared for, don't worry."

There was a knock at the door, and Ted Vanderberg stuck his head around the door. His eyes grew big, and he smiled when he saw Eliso was awake. "Thank God, man. May I come in?"

"Of course, Teddy."

Ted pulled up a chair. "Stone and Nan have taken Ettie home for a few hours. They've been here pretty much twenty-four-seven, but Stone insisted Nan and the baby get some rest. They'll be back later."

Eliso felt a wave of gratitude towards his best friend. Stone had always been there for him, and he knew now would be no different. He nodded at Ted. "How does it feel to be an uncle, Teddy?"

Ted smiled, his face softening. "Incredible... I admit, I wasn't Nan's biggest fan to begin with—mostly my fault—I acted like an ass at Dad's funeral. But Ettie? Wow, man. Kind of makes me broody."

Eliso smiled, but the weight of his grief was beginning to bear down hard on him, and the thought that his future, the one he had planned with Beulah, the love of his life, had been smashed into billion pieces was unbearable. He was broken and he knew—he could never be fixed.

Fenella seemed to sense he needed time alone. "Hey, Teddy, let's give Eli some room, and go grab some coffee. Right?"

"Sure thing." Ted squeezed Eliso's arm. "You need anything, buddy, you give me a call, okay?"

Eliso nodded, but breathed a sigh of relief when he was alone. He wanted to wallow in his devastation. *Mio Dio, Beulah, my love, my life, I failed you... I didn't protect you. I'm so sorry... I love you...*

... I'll love you forever.

CHAPTER SIXTEEN

Nan woke, stiff and feeling grubby, but comfortable on Stone's huge bed. He'd draped a knitted, snuggly throw over her, and now she pushed it away and got up. From the living room she heard Stone's low voice and Ettie's happy gurgling. She went to the door and watched them for a few moments. Stone was tickling his daughter who was wriggling and making happy noises. Nan's heart went out to them. She couldn't quite believe the week they had just had.

Stone had moved her and Ettie into his apartment, and Nan had been staggered by the ease of it. Within hours, he'd turned one room into a nursery with everything a baby could want. He'd even had it decorated in pale, soothing colors, installing a gorgeous (and Nan knew, *expensive*) crib, a day bed, a rocking chair for her to feed Ettie in, and credenzas full of every essential item he could think of as the final touch.

Nan had been staggered and a little discombobulated. From a man who told her he never wanted children—to this? Stone had picked Ettie up now and was hugging her to his big chest. Ettie reached out with her star-like tiny fingers and touched his face.

"You look so good together," Nan said softly, and Stone looked up and smiled at her.

"Hey, beautiful, did you sleep okay?"

She nodded and went to them, stroking Ettie's dark head. Her daughter was blinking at her, sleepy now. Nan kissed her forehead. "I did, thank you, but I could do with a shower. She needs feeding first."

Stone handed her the child, and Nan unbuttoned her shirt. She smiled at him as Ettie began to feed. "This doesn't bother you? The whole Madonna/whore complex passed you by?"

"I've never believed in that," Stone said now, stroking his daughter's cheek. "What? Suddenly a woman becomes undesirable because she's a mother? Bullshit. *Oops.*" He looked guilty and Nan grinned.

"I think we're okay with the cussing until she starts to speak."

"Sorry." He chuckled and leaned over to kiss her. "Anyway, what I was saying was… that you need to feed my child doesn't make me want you any less, quite the opposite." He nuzzled her nose. "Really, I couldn't want you more, Nan Songbird."

She kissed him and smiled. "Well, after she's asleep, I need to bathe… want to join me in the shower?"

"How about a long, hot soak in the tub?"

She moaned. "God, that sounds so good."

"In the meantime, you hungry? Thirsty?"

"A cup of decaf tea would be perfect."

"You got it."

AFTER ETTIE WAS FED and was sound asleep in her new crib, Nan and Stone stripped each other slowly and stepped into his huge tub. Stone wrapped his arms around her. "I love you, Nanouk Songbird."

"I love you, too. Listen, I've been thinking, we should think about Ettie's name... would you want her to have your last name?"

Stone kissed her temple. "Well, obviously, but at the same time, she's existed in the world as Ettie Songbird for nearly five months now. And it is a beautiful name as it is, so I'm of two minds about it."

Nan turned around and faced him. "I think so, too... but I want you in there somewhere, so I wondered how you would feel about having Janie as her middle name? After your sister?"

Stone looked taken aback and then moved beyond words. "Wow. Every day you surprise me more, baby. That would be incredible. A real tribute to Janie's memory, thank you."

"You're welcome, my darling. Tell me more about her—you told me how she passed, but not much about who she was."

Stone ran his hands through Nan's long hair. "She was a lot like you—she and I had a special bond. She was a lot younger, too. I was already twelve when Janie was born; Ted was nine. Janie was a tomboy, too, always climbing trees when she was told not to, always laughing. Just a ball of fun." His face clouded over. "The day she died... I had a paper to write for a class, and I was in a bad mood. I told her I couldn't play with her, and she was sulking. She went to find Ted, and they went out to the beach to play. An hour later, Ted came screaming back to the house, saying Janie had gone into the ocean and he couldn't find her. They found her body twelve days later, washed up along the coast."

"God, how awful. Ted must have been devastated."

Stone nodded. "I don't think he's ever forgiven himself, but, jeez, he was a kid, what was he supposed to do?"

Nan kissed him. "I'm so sorry, baby." She sighed. "I can't imagine what Eliso is going through."

"It's unthinkable." Stone's arms tightened around her as he drew her close. "If anything ever happened to you... God."

"It won't. We'll catch this asshole and make sure he rots in jail. He won't hurt anyone else."

Stone's fingertips were trailing up and down her spine, making her shiver with pleasure. Stone gazed at her. "For the next few hours, let's pretend nothing bad has ever happened in the world."

Nan nodded, her eyes dark with desire. "Good idea." Her lips met his, and fire exploded through her body. Her breasts, her nipples rock hard, pressed against his chest, her belly against his as she straddled him, and she felt his cock twitch and harden. She rubbed her groin against his. "Fuck me hard, Vanderberg."

Stone grinned and lifted her, impaling her on his huge cock. Nan sighed happily as he filled her, and they began to move together, both watching his cock sliding in and out of her. "God, I love to fuck you, Nan, our bodies fit together so well."

"Made for each other."

"You know it... now, harder, baby, harder..."

Nan began to thrust harder onto him, feeling him go deeper as Stone slipped a hand between her legs to rub her clit. "That's it, beautiful, give yourself to me."

Nan closed her eyes and let her head drop back. Stone pressed his lips to her throat. "You're so fucking beautiful, Nanouk, so very, very fuckable... I want to have you in every way tonight."

The friction of his cock in her cunt and his fingers on her clit was making her wild. "Tell me, tell me what you want to do to me."

Stone gave a low growl. "I want to fuck you so hard you can't walk straight in the morning, suck on your clit until you scream, bite at your nipples until you beg me to stop, tongue fuck your bellybutton because I know you like that. I can make you come in so many ways, beautiful girl..."

Nan gasped and cried out as she came, feeling a rush of wet

warmth flood inside her, her vagina clenching around his cock as he thrust harder. Stone grinned as she tried to catch her breath. "You know what? I'm going to fuck you from behind while I press you up against the window, let the whole of Manhattan see the most beautiful woman in the world when she comes."

Nan was so turned on by his dirty talk that she bit down on his shoulder, making him groan.

"Wild tiger woman."

He kept his promise, fucking her from behind up against the ceiling to floor window in the living room, then taking her to his bed and reaming her into submission until they were both exhausted. They fell asleep in each other's arms only waking when they heard someone buzzing at the intercom.

"I HOPE I haven't interrupted anything," Ted said as his brother let him in. Stone hugged him.

"No, we were just sleeping. Come on in. God, is it eight P.M. already?"

Ted chuckled. "Yeah, the days have been kind of running together lately. I've just been at the hospital. Eliso is awake."

Stone stopped. "He is?"

"Yeah, and the docs say he's doing fine, but he needs rest. That's what I came to tell you. They said no more visitors tonight."

Stone sighed but nodded. "Okay. Look, want some coffee?"

"Love some."

"Hey."

They both turned at the sound of Nan's voice. Her robe pulled tight around her, she moved towards Stone, giving a wary glance at Ted. They had only met a few times since that awkward first meeting, and Nan still wasn't sure about Stone's brother. He gave her a friendly smile now though.

"Hey, Nan, how are you?"

"Good, thanks. Well, as good as any of us are, under the circumstances."

Ted's smile faded. "I know. I've never seen anyone as broken as Eliso, it's horrible. He was talking about leaving the country, retiring from film, exiling himself. I think he was just rambling; he's on some pretty strong drugs, but still."

"We can't let him torture himself. There was nothing he could have done. Someone is targeting him, and we have to find out why." Stone's voice was hard, and Nan nodded.

"Agreed."

Ted cleared his throat. "Also, I have to warn you, the press is all over this—every angle." He gave Nan an apologetic look. "And they're onto the both of you: your relationship, Ettie..."

"Oh, goddamn it."

"Yeah. Some of the gutter press are trying to make out that this is some kind of sex circle you all had going on, and that Beulah was killed in some kind of kinky knife play game."

"What the actual fuck?" Nan was incensed. "How dare they?"

"They want to sell their disgusting rags, baby, so they'll make shit up. Ignore it. We're all adults, and most of the world knows none of it is true."

Nan seethed, and Stone drew her into his arms. "All that matters is that we're together, and that we're safe. Ted, was the security at the hospital set up like we discussed?"

"Yup. No one's getting near Eli or Fen or Beulah's parents." He sighed. "This is such a weird situation. I mean, Eliso's probably one of the easiest going guys in the film industry; he doesn't have any enemies."

"We all know how obsessive people can get over movie

stars." Stone sounded exhausted. "We have to believe the police will find him—or her."

"You think a woman could do this?" Ted looked surprised, and Nan gave a cynical laugh.

"We're just as capable, believe me. Although, thankfully, it doesn't happen as much." She rubbed her face. "I can't stop thinking about Beulah. How can that much... force of personality be snuffed out?"

"We'll never know the answer to that."

All three of them sat in silence for a moment before Nan got up. "I'm going to look in on Tee-Tee."

As she passed Ted, he caught her hand. "Nan, I just wanted to say... the first time we met, I was an a-hole. I'm sorry. I hope we can be friends."

Nan gave him a smile. "Of course. This week has shown us all that petty arguments are just not worth it."

ETTIE WAS AWAKE, but quietly sucking on her thumb. Nan gently removed it from her daughter's mouth. "I thought we'd made an agreement on thumb sucking, Tee-Tee."

She grinned as she picked her daughter up, then made a face. "Someone's made a stinky."

As she cleaned her daughter up and changed her diaper, she blew raspberries on her little tummy and made Ettie gurgle with delight. Holding her close, she kissed her. "You are the best thing in this world, Tee-Tee, the very best."

"Seconded."

Nan felt Stone wrap his arms around them both and pressed his lips to her temple. "Has Ted gone?"

"Yeah, he's bushed. Looks like it's just the three of us for this evening."

Nan leaned back against him. "That sounds perfect."

. . .

They spent a blissful evening, eating, playing with Ettie and talking before heading to bed. "Look at us all domesticated," Nan joked, and Stone laughed, shaking his head.

"If some of my exes could see me now."

Nan slid into the cool Egyptian cotton sheets. "Just how many exes have you had?"

Stone laughed. "You really want to know?"

Nan considered. "Actually, no, I don't. I just need to know there isn't any other woman right now."

Stone drew her to him and make her look him in the eyes. "There is, and will never be, anyone else for me. I found my home when I met you, Nanouk."

She flushed with pleasure. "Sweet talker. God, doesn't France seem a million miles away?"

Stone grinned. "Well, if we're being pedantic, about four thousand."

She giggled and punched his shoulder. "Shut up. But, seriously, so, so much has happened between now and then. I just wish whoever it was tormenting Eliso was caught, and he was safe."

"Me too, baby, me too."

"Flowers?"

Eliso looked bemused as the nurse carried the huge bouquet into his room. No one he knew would send him *flowers*, surely? The nurse handed him the card with a smile.

He opened it and recoiled with a shock. With a shaking hand, he picked up the photograph that had fallen from the envelope.

Beulah. Dead. Her beautiful body torn apart by a knife, her eyes open and staring, terror on her face. Blood.

"*Mio Dio, mio Dio...*" Eliso turned the photograph over and somehow, his world became even more terrifying. On the back, three words were written in black ink, and Eliso knew this horror wasn't over. Three words.

Everyone you love.

CHAPTER SEVENTEEN

Nan stared unhappily at the huge security guards who escorted her into her law firm on a Monday morning a few weeks later. She shot an apologetic look at her personal assistant, who was unhappy that the security team was scouring the office for weapons, bombs, bugs... who knew what else?

Since Eliso had received the threat, he and Stone had gone into overdrive, ratcheting up security for everyone who'd even *breathed* near them in the last twenty years and not taking 'no' for an answer. Only Ted had pushed back, telling Stone he'd hire his own bodyguards. "No argument but let me find my own. I have to meet with a bunch of studio honchos this week about the offers that are coming in for Eliso, and I'd rather have my own people around me."

Stone hadn't been happy but knew he couldn't force Ted to take his help. "Fine, but Teddy, please... I already lost one sibling."

It had been the wrong thing to say to Ted, who looked away. Nan had been the one to save the situation. "He wasn't blaming you, Ted. He didn't mean it like that."

Stone realized how his words must have sounded then and hated to see his brother look so stricken. "I really wasn't blaming you, Teddy. I misspoke and I'm sorry."

Ted had been delighted when Nan told him they were giving Ettie his lost sister's name. "That's so beautiful." He looked moved to tears and Nan hugged him. Their relationship had improved so much in the last few weeks that she barely recognized him as the angry, spiteful man she'd met at his father's funeral.

She had also been building a friendship with Stone and Ted's mother, Diana. Silver-haired and effortlessly elegant, Diana Vanderberg had been the daughter of the family scion, Ward Vanderberg, the money behind the throne. A throwback to the days of Jackie Kennedy, she dressed chicly, usually in Chanel or Givenchy, especially when hosting charity galas or lunches at her mansion, but when she came to visit with Nan and her granddaughter, she dressed down—for *her*.

"I'm sure those jeans cost more than my yearly salary," Nan muttered to an amused Stone, as they watched Diana and Ettie play with poster paints, with the child sticking her hands all over her grandmother's designer jeans. Diana didn't seem to care.

Diana had listened to Nan's story, about why she hadn't told Stone about Ettie, and had sympathized. "I think you did the only thing you could," she told Nan, and Nan was relieved the older woman didn't hold the past against her.

Indeed, she was delighted to find out that Diana had known her mother. "We held several functions at the Oyster Bay library—Genevieve worked there, I understand?"

Nan had nodded proudly. "She ran the place like clockwork. My elder sister Etta worked there, too."

"How wonderful." Diana studied her. "Stone told me you

were on your own for a long time. Let me just say, Nanouk, that you are a part of our family now."

Now, back at work, Ettie safely at home with Diana and their massive security guard—Nan didn't care that it was overkill, she wanted her daughter safe—she felt as if she could give her job her full attention. Alan called her into his office as soon as he heard she was in.

"Some news from the police. They say they are looking at the possibility that Beulah was the target all along."

Nan sighed. "That could be it, but I think, if someone was obsessed with Beulah... they would have killed Eliso, too. Plus, the threat he received was directed at *him*."

"I agree, but they have to check." Alan sat back in his chair. "We also have to consider that it could be someone close to Eliso."

"Like?"

"His sister. Stone. Stone's family members—Ted is Eliso's manager, after all."

Nan shook her head. "I can speak for all of them. Well, Stone's family at least."

"Nan... maybe you should recuse yourself from this case. You're too close to it, to Eliso, to the Vanderbergs. Can you honestly tell me you're impartial?"

Nan's body slumped in defeat. "You know what? You're right. I'm not, I'm *not* impartial. I can't be. These people are, astonishingly, my family now. Every night I close my eyes, and I imagine Beulah's terror, her pain. I see the depth of Eliso's heartbreak. I see the fear in Stone's eyes which is a mirror of my own that the killer will get to Ettie." She felt tears threatening, and Alan reached across the desk and took her hand.

"Look, while this is going on, take a sabbatical. Paid, of course. You should be with your family."

"You don't have to pay me," she said but Alan waved her away.

"Take the time. Be with your daughter, Nan. Come back after this is all over."

NAN WAS DRIVEN BACK to Stone's apartment building, and she knew she was doing the right thing. A weight lifted from her shoulders. She would have time now to do her own research, without the need to check in with Alan, albeit from a laptop in a *fortress*. She smiled at her two burly security guards as they drove her underground to the garage under the building. "Babysitting duty suiting you, boys?"

One of them, Greg, grinned. "Just doing our jobs, Ms. Songbird."

As they got out of the car, Nan was about to ask him if he was ex-military when she heard the shout. Her name being called.

"Nan!"

As she turned, aware of Greg and the other guard Simon reacting sharply to the sound, Nan saw in horror Duggan Smollett stumbling towards her, eyes wild, a gun aimed directly at her.

Time froze for a second and then Greg was shoving her back into the car as Duggan Smollett opened fire.

GUNFIRE and the squeal of tires. More shouting. Greg on top of her, protecting her with his body. Then silence.

"Greg? Greg, are you okay, were you hit?"

"No, ma'am. Stay down. Stay down."

It was dark inside the car under Greg's big body. She heard

Simon shout something, and the weight lifted as Greg shifted and let her sit up.

"Get Ms. Songbird to safety then we'll deal with... this."

With Greg gripping her upper arm tightly, Nan was rushed to the elevator. As the doors closed, she saw him. Duggan. Pinned to the wall by a black Audi, blood spattered across the concrete. Dead.

"What the hell happened?"

Greg was amped up. "Mr. Vanderberg hit him with his car. Trapped him. Simon got off a shot, but it was Mr. Vanderberg that stopped him. He's waiting for the police below."

Something didn't add up, but for a moment Nan couldn't place what. "How the hell did Duggan Smollett get in here?"

Greg's face was grim. "That's what we need to know. When we get to our floor, I need you to stay inside the elevator until I tell you it's clear, understood?"

Nan, frightened and shocked, nodded. At the penthouse level, Greg got out, his gun drawn. In a couple of seconds, he was back. "All clear. Thanks for waiting."

Nan walked into the apartment to see Diana, her blue eyes wide with concern. "What's wrong?" She was holding Ettie, who had picked up on the tension, and reached out toward her mother.

Nan took her and held her close, taking a couple of deep breaths before she told Diana what happened. Diana looked shaken. "And Ted stopped him?"

That was it. That was the thing Nan hadn't understood. Stone drove a Lotus, *Ted* had the black Audi. She looked to Greg for confirmation. He nodded. "Yup. Mr. Edward Vanderberg drove his car at Smollett. Killed him, thank God."

Nan shook her head. "I just don't understand... I thought the thing with Duggan was over and done with in Cannes, last year.

Why would he try to kill me now, and how the hell did he get in?"

"We'll have to wait until the police investigate, I think."

A FEW MOMENTS LATER, Ted arrived, flanked by a detective and some uniformed officers. Diana hugged her son, followed by Nan. "Thank you," she whispered in his ear. "You saved my life."

Ted shook his head. "Anyone would have done the same. Listen, the police want your statement. Has anyone called Stone?"

"Called Stone about what?"

They turned at the sound of his voice, and they were surprised to see an exhausted Eliso standing by his side.

"Look who came to visit." Stone grinned at his friend, but Nan could see the other man was drooping.

"Eli, come sit down with me." She made him sit next to her and held his hand. Looking back at Stone, she tried to smile. "While it's wonderful to see you both, we have some disturbing news."

STONE DIDN'T FEEL JUST anger, he felt *rage*. Rage towards Duggan Smollett and rage towards himself for not making sure Smollett could never get near Nan again. *Why now, for Chrissakes?*

"Something tells me he was set up," Nan was saying, and Stone bugged at her.

"Nan, that man tried to gut you last year, now he tries to shoot you, and you think he was set up?"

She nodded, her large brown eyes wide and frightened. "I don't believe he's Beulah's killer. I don't. Why? He didn't know her; hell, I didn't know her when Duggan was around at Cannes. I think he was sent as a decoy."

"Yes, but by *whom*?" Stone realized he and Nan were the only ones talking in a room full of statues. He looked at Greg. "And I want you to fire the people on guard duty in the garage."

"Already done, boss," Greg nodded at him. "We also moved the paparazzi outside back, told them we would personally 'deal' with any of them who tried to get in. Police are backing us up."

"Greg dove on top of me when Duggan started shooting, baby," Nan said in a soft voice, getting up and coming to him. He held her tightly. The thought of coming home to find her shot dead... *God*.

He looked over her head and nodded gratefully at Greg. "Thank you, Greg, I couldn't have asked for any more. Are the police sure Smollett is dead?"

"Very sure." Ted looked as shell-shocked as the rest of them. "I have to go downtown to the station to give my statement—there might be charges, but I'd do the same thing again."

"Charges?" Nan pulled away from Stone, her expression astonished. "Charges for saving lives? Bull crap, I'll go with you, I'll tell them..."

"Nan, calm down, it's a formality. No one is going to charge Teddy with anything."

Stone saw Nan draw in a deep breath. Eliso, sitting quietly on the couch, spoke up.

"This has to end. No more bloodshed. Teddy, can you set up a television interview for me?"

They all looked at Eliso who nodded. "I want to address the killer directly. Ask him what he wants to make this all stop. Money, power... whatever it takes. I won't see anyone else hurt." He winced in pain, and Stone went to his friend. "Eli, go lay down in one of the guest rooms. I'm not even sure the hospital should have discharged you."

"I will if Teddy does what I ask."

Ted nodded. "I'll set it up, Eli. Just, please, take care of yourself."

When Eliso had gone into the guest room and shut the door, Nan picked up Ettie and hugged her. If Duggan's bullets had found their mark, she would have never seen her beloved daughter or the man she loved again. She had to acknowledge—she was scared. Terrified. "We are all in danger, clearly," she said, "so what are we going to do about it?"

"Eli's idea is a good one," Ted said carefully, waiting for Stone to object. When he didn't, Ted nodded and got up. "Look, I think we should all get out of Manhattan. Maybe hole up somewhere where we can be sure we're safe."

Stone shook his head. "That I disagree with. If we sequester ourselves in some out of the way place where the police can't get to us quickly…"

Ted shrugged. "You have a point. God, Stone, I just want the people we care about safe. I saw the crime scene photos of what this guy did to Beulah." He glanced at Nan and Nan saw Stone pale.

"I have no clue what's right, but for now, we stay here, agreed?"

Ted left shortly after with the police, and Diane offered to put Ettie down for her nap. Nan and Stone went to their room to talk, but both of them soon fell silent. Stone's arms were cradling Nan, and she rested her head against his chest for a moment before looking up at him.

"I hate this."

"I know." Stone pressed his lips to her forehead. "The

thought of Duggan going after you, of anyone going after you... I can't imagine what Eli's going through right now."

"He's shattered; you can see it in his eyes. There's no life there." Nan winced at her poorly chosen words. "You know what I mean."

"I do." Stone tilted her chin up, so he could kiss her. "I love you so much, it kills me to even think what Eli must be feeling."

"Stone?"

"Yeah, baby?"

"For the next few hours, make the world go away."

He kissed her again, this time with more passion, pouring all the fear and terror he felt into the kiss. He snagged the belt of her wrap dress in his finger and pulled it open, pushing the fabric aside to kiss her skin.

On her back, Nan stroked his dark head as he kissed her stomach, her belly, and, as he drew her panties down her legs, his mouth found her clit and she sighed, letting all the angst of the day go as she concentrated on the sensations Stone was sending through her body.

Stone pushed her thighs apart as his tongue sought to delve deep into her cunt, its quick, stabbing motions making her body shiver with pleasure. "I want you inside me," she whispered, and Stone moved up the bed to kiss her mouth.

"Every part of you is heaven," he murmured against her mouth as he unzipped himself and freed his cock from his jeans. "Every single inch of you."

He hitched her legs around his waist and thrust into her, his cock rock-hard and relentless as they fucked. *How could I ever have thought I could live without this man?* Nan kissed him, her mouth hungry on his, her hands on his solid back, fingers digging through his still unopened shirt.

Stone's eyes never left hers as he made her come, groaning

through his own orgasm, shooting thick creamy cum deep into her belly.

Nan helped him undress fully afterward, and they made love again, this time taking their time, kissing and caressing each other. As Nan shivered and moaned through another orgasm, Stone smiled down at her. "Marry me," he whispered, and Nan didn't hesitate.

"Yes," she said, nodding, her eyes serious. "Yes, I will marry you, Stone Vanderberg."

What she didn't know was that the delight in his eyes would soon thereafter be replaced by fear, terror, and grief.

And that more than one of them would be fighting for their lives.

18

CHAPTER EIGHTEEN

Eliso had removed the bandage from his head for the interview, showing the jagged wound on the side of the head with the still bright purple bruises. He wanted to show off what the killer had done to him, and to tell the interviewer, a kind-hearted elder statesman of the news channel, what exactly had been done to Beulah. He wanted to shock and to goad the killer. He wanted...

He wanted Beulah alive and in his arms. When Nan and Stone had quietly announced they were going to get married, he had been delighted for his friends—and heartbroken, remembering that wonderful and terrible night Beulah proposed to him. He still saw the delight on her beautiful face, still felt her skin under his fingertips.

Still smelled her blood. Still saw the horrific wounds the killer inflicted on her, even before he'd heard her scream.

Butchered. That was the word he was going to use. Beulah had been butchered.

Eliso closed his eyes, the harsh studio lights burning into his brain, making his head scream with pain. He felt a hand on his arm. Fenella.

She had been his rock since Beulah's murder, and she put her arm around him now. She spoke a few words of comfort in Italian to him and then rested her head against his, careful not to hurt him. "Eliso, we are all here for you."

The interviewer, Bob Jenkins, arrived then and shook his hand. "I'm so sorry for your loss, Mr. Patini."

"Eliso, please, and thank you."

Bob let the assistant put his microphone on before speaking again. "Eliso, the floor is yours. Anything and everything you want to talk about. Obviously, we can't have explicit bad language but..."

Eliso gave a mirthless snort of laughter. "No cussing, but talking about a woman being gutted is palatable for the American audience."

Bob nodded sagely. "Yep, it's just as fucked up as it sounds."

Eliso appreciated the man's candor. "Fine. No bad language."

"We're going live in five, people," the stage manager called. Fenella kissed her brother's forehead and walked out of shot.

"Be nice to him," she warned Bob, who nodded at her and smiled.

"She's feisty."

"You have no idea." Eliso liked this man; he was warm and had a no-nonsense air about him.

"We're on in sixty seconds."

Eliso took a sip of water from the glass next to him, and his hand trembled so much he splashed water onto his lap.

"Hey," Bob said quietly, "You can do this. You know how to do this, man. This is in your blood. It's okay to feel nervous, but don't forget the reason you're here. I got your back."

Eliso smiled gratefully at him, and as the countdown began, and Bob spoke his intro into the camera, Eliso switched into performance mode. Bob was right—performing was in Eliso's blood—just this time, there was no character to hide behind.

Eliso steeled himself for the first question—and waited.

"HE'S DOING REALLY WELL." Stone's apartment was full of people all watching the huge flat screen television as Eliso talked about what had happened. Eliso's parents, Diana, their huge security team, and Nan sat on the couches watching Eliso's every reaction or expression. Ted was at the studio with Eliso and Fen. Nan was the one who spoke first. "He's doing really well. He's holding it together."

She was holding Eliso's mother's hand and could feel the other woman trembling. She squeezed her hand. "He's doing great, Lucia, really great."

Stone had invited Beulah's parents, but they had wanted to go back to England. Beulah had been buried there as Eliso had wanted—he hated the fact that there was even a question—he felt like he didn't have the right to say where her body would lie. "I can always come to London," he told them, "For me, it's important she is near her family."

Nan wondered at his generosity in the face of his overwhelming grief. She would look at Ettie and at Stone and wonder if she, too, could be that generous. Diana Vanderberg had already lost one child through tragedy. Nan closed her eyes, feeling sick. The thought of losing Ettie was too much to bear, and yet both Diana and the Tegans had experienced it. Their strength was an inspiration.

They watched as Eliso described the events of that night, his face lighting up when he talked about Beulah's proposal, their joy, their happiness. He talked about the two elderly women he had been talking to and the way he kept in touch with them still.

As Bob Jenkins pressed him on the horror that followed, Nan saw the slump of Eliso's shoulders and wanted to hug him tightly. *Such a sweet man,* she thought. *For this to happen to such a wonderful, kind, warm man... it was unthinkable. Who the hell would want to torment Eliso Patini?*

She felt tears pricking her eyes and had to turn away from Eliso's mother. Eliso wasn't the man he was even a month ago. Even his physical appearance, his distinctive dark curls half-shaved off on one side where his surgery scar was, was off to her.

Nan's cell phone rang, and she excused herself to answer it. It wasn't a number she recognized. "Hello?"

"Ms. Songbird?"

Ugh. Miles Kirke. "What do you want, Kirke? This isn't a good time."

"I'm sorry to disturb. I know this must be a horrible time for you and Mr. Patini. I heard about the attempted shooting... and I want to apologize for my behavior the last time we met."

Something in Kirke's voice piqued Nan's attention. "Okay." What was this about?

"Ms. Songbird... can we meet? I believe I may have found out something about Duggan Smollett's *benefactor*, for want of a better word, but it's sensitive. I hesitate to ask you to meet in private, given how I behaved last time. But... I think this could be the answer to what's happening to Mr. Patini."

Nan was silent for a long moment. "Why should I believe you?" She asked him eventually.

"I don't blame you for thinking the worst of me, I don't. Listen, I'm happy for you to bring a personal guard with you, but I can't be seen to meet with you in public."

"I need more than that."

Kirke sighed and when he spoke again, he lowered his voice. "I don't believe Mr. Patini is the target of this campaign."

Nan felt a cold hand of fear close around her heart. "Then who?"

A long pause. "Mr Vanderberg."

No. No...

Nan took a deep breath in and closed her eyes. "Where and when should I meet you, Mr. Kirke? I need to know everything you do."

CHAPTER NINETEEN

He was close, *so* close to getting what he had always wanted. From birth almost, or at least since he was three or four years old, he had known about and understood the unlimited potential of his psychopathy and the utter lack of empathy inside him, and he knew that nothing could be denied to him.

He killed from a young age—hell, he enjoyed it—especially when it was a beautiful woman, helpless underneath his knife, or pressed up against his gun.

The knife was easier—no gunpowder or bullet evidence. He would use it, then drop it into the Hudson, no problem, buy another one on the internet, have it delivered to a forwarding address.

He'd paid Ruthie to take possession of the knives until she had ratted to Nan about the junkie he'd hired to attack Eliso.

Both Willa Green and Ruthie had died quickly. The Tegan woman had tried to fight him until he had debilitated her with his blade, then when pretty-boy Eliso was out of action, he stabbed her over and over, relishing every moment.

I am an animal. It was his mantra. But soon, he would have what he always wanted. Stone. Stone would be so grateful that he had managed to save his young daughter that it wouldn't be a question—they would be together. Stone's grief over Nan's murder would also break him down, making him more vulnerable.

God, he couldn't *wait*. When they found her body, together he decided, he would be Stone's... rock. *Ha!*

He thought of Nan now, so beautiful, so loving and soft. He had dreamed about this, about her blood on his hands, her lovely eyes full of agony and terror as he killed her, the light going out in them as she died. It was so close he could taste it.

In the next twenty-four hours, Nanouk Songbird would be dead, and Stone would at last, be his.

CHAPTER TWENTY

Nan was apprehensive about meeting Kirke, but she had to know why he thought Stone was the target of the killer's campaign. None of it made any sense.

Still she managed to convince Stone that she needed to go out to get some things for Ettie, and he made her take Greg with her. In the car, she told Greg where they were going. He looked unsure. "Ms. Songbird, I have very specific orders."

"Look, normally, I wouldn't ask. But this lawyer has some information regarding the case that could affect Stone, and I don't want to wait. Please, Greg."

She eventually persuaded him, and he drove her out to the meeting place, outside the city. Kirke's home was a palatial mansion, but after she and Greg went inside, she found it cold and drafty. She wondered if Kirke was married, but as she looked at the décor, she decided not. It was all too... male.

"Ms. Songbird, thank you for coming." Miles Kirke shook her hand and nodded to Greg. "Maybe I ask you to wait outside the room, sir?"

Greg looked at Nan, who nodded. In her purse, she had a

can of pepper spray that Ted had given her that morning, and her entire body was on alert.

Kirke didn't look like the same arrogant man she had last seen; rather, his pallor was clammy, and he looked nervous, his small eyes darting about quickly. He asked her to sit, but as she chose a chair closest to the huge window, he suddenly grabbed her and steered her away. Nan froze as his hands touched her shoulders, and he let her go immediately, holding his hands up.

"Sorry, sorry, just... not near the window, please."

Oh, boy. Kirke's paranoia was almost laughable—but also catching. Nan sat as far away from him as possible, but away from the window. Kirke himself sat across from her.

"Mr. Kirke, you said you thought Stone was the real target of Beulah Tegan's killer... please, tell me what you know."

Kirke took a deep breath in. Even with the obvious fear he was feeling, he wanted to perform, Nan thought. "Ms. Songbird..."

"Call me Nan, would you?" Nan said irritably, and Kirke nodded.

"Miles. Nan, it began as a theory after my case against Eliso Patini collapsed. As you can imagine, I did my research on the man and found, remarkably, that he simply has no enemies, no one who would want to do this. Even his stalkers—as you can imagine, a man who looks like Patini has had a few—were pretty *milquetoast* compared to this. So, my range of investigation widened—and I found something. Did you know about Mr. Vanderberg's sister?"

Nan nodded, frowning. "Janie. Yes, of course. She drowned."

Kirke chewed his lip. "That's the official story, yes. But I dug deeper, and although this isn't admissible in court, I was able to gain access to some sealed records. Jane Vanderberg was murdered."

Nan felt like the ground was coming up to meet her. "What?"

"It was hushed up, and the suspect..."

"Ted?" Nan whispered, and Kirke nodded. She leaned forward, trying not to scream.

"His father knew about it—I don't know about the mother, but Vanderberg Senior had the power and connections to get it hushed up. Janie was cremated soon after she was found to hide her injuries, but they are listed in the medical examiner's report. The *unofficial* coroner's report, obviously."

"How did she die?" Nan felt sick.

"Stabbed. Multiple times. They think he used a sharp stone, but he used so much force that some of her ribs were broken."

"Jesus Christ." Nan gagged, and Kirke got up and poured her some water.

"I'd offer you something stronger, but I know you might be, you know..." He colored, nodded at her chest, and for the first time, she felt gratitude towards Kirke.

"Thank you. Look, Miles, I hate to say this, but I believe it. The first time I met Ted, he was... *off*, and I thought it was just because he was grieving for his father."

"Ah yes, his father. Died from acute poisoning."

"What? I didn't know that."

"The police in Oyster Bay didn't pursue it, but tell me this... Ted took his parents to dinner at one of those trendy raw food places—for the first time. Now, Ted is a known-gastronome, and he loves his steak. *Loves*. Owns three grills in his huge backyard, all state-of-the art."

Nan nodded. "I know, we've eaten with him." She was confused now. "Get to the point, would you?"

"Why would a man who has never in his life—by his own account—eaten at a vegetarian restaurant, suddenly want to take his parents to a raw food place?"

Nan wasn't getting it. "I have no idea."

Miles smirked a little, and she saw the old arrogance creep back in. "If you eat with him again, don't have the mushrooms."

Nan stared at him and suddenly she smiled. "You're kidding."

"I'm afraid not."

"No, really, this is something like out of a bad movie. Kid sneaks a poison mushroom into his dad's salad? Come *on.*"

"I would say it was one of Ted's kinder murders."

"Murders as in plural?"

Kirke stood up. "A year ago, in Cannes, did you see Ted there?"

She shook her head.

"But he *was* there—I've seen the credit card receipts. Eliso, Stone, they had no idea he was watching them. He was planning to destroy Eliso."

"But why? That's what I don't get. Why?"

"Don't you get it? He's obsessed with his brother. He doesn't want to share—he never has. *Ever.* He killed his sister, so he would continue to have Stone to himself."

Nan shook her head. "Okay, so we know for a fact he killed Janie, and that he's an asshole, but I don't understand targeting Eliso."

"Stone loves Eliso Patini like a brother. More like a brother than Ted." Miles' voice was gentle. "Can you deny it? Think of how Stone is with Ted and Eliso."

Nan closed her eyes. What Miles said made sense, but it sounded too incredible to believe. But she went through the history of seeing Stone and Eliso together, and Stone and Ted together—and Miles was right. Stone and Eliso were inseparable. Blood brothers.

"Fuck." She whispered, and Miles looked sympathetic.

"Twisted, I know, and honestly, I'm praying to all hell that I'm wrong."

Nan glanced at the windows. "Those bulletproof?"

Miles nodded. "Newly installed this morning, and I'm not just being paranoid. Last night my offices were broken into, and the files I had collated on Ted Vanderberg went missing. Since I came by them, let's say, *unofficially*, I can't go to the police. Which means Ted knows I'm digging up evidence against him. He'll kill me without even thinking about it." He studied her. "He's going to kill you, Nan. I guarantee that son-of-a-bitch is already planning your murder. He's obsessed with his brother."

"Why hasn't he killed his mother? Why just his dad?"

"Maybe dear old dad was going to blow the whistle on him? I don't know. All I know is that the only reason Eliso Patini is still alive is that he makes big bank for Ted. A dead actor can't do that—a living breathing actor wracked with grief is sympathetic and will bring in the roles and the cash. Look for Oscar nominations in Patini's future just because his hot girlfriend was murdered. It's the way Hollywood works—not that I have to tell you that."

"What about Duggan Smollett?"

"What about him? After you got him fired in France, he had trouble getting work. Sheila Maffey got him blacklisted. Did Ted know about him?"

Nan thought back for a moment then groaned. "Yes. I told him how Stone and I met—and he'd pissed me off, so I gave him the whole truth."

"Find it funny Smollett came after you only *after* you'd met Ted?"

Fuck. Nan was angry now. "That son of a bitch."

"He was trying to throw you all off his scent. He knew someone was sniffing around his past. Didn't work out the way Ted wanted it to."

"No. I told them all I didn't think Duggan killed Beulah. Goddamn it, why didn't I think?"

"How would you know?"

She smiled at him sadly. "I used to pride myself on following my gut instincts."

"No one could make this stuff up, Nan. Don't beat yourself up." He crossed his legs, having relaxed a little. "You have incredible potential as a lawyer, Nan. The DA's office would be very interested to hear from you once you have a little more experience."

"Thank you, I appreciate that." Nan rubbed her face. "Now what do I do?"

"Go home, talk to Stone, keep him and your child the hell away from Ted. After that... I wish I knew."

IN THE CAR on the way back to the city, Nan went through everything Miles had suggested. The heavy weight of dread in her chest told her he was right—how could he not be?

Jesus. Nothing as fucked up as families. Her phone bleeped with a message, and she opened it.

Her eyes saw only in tunnel-vision, and the breath froze in her lungs. A photo message. A selfie.

Ted, smiling into the camera, holding a crying Ettie. On the message he'd written.

HI MOMMY! *We're going on an adventure!*

EVERYTHING IN NAN'S world stopped.

CHAPTER TWENTY-ONE

Her phone rang, and she saw Ted was calling her. "You son-of-a-bitch!"

Ted laughed. "Now, don't be so mean, Mommy. Listen to me, everything will be okay. Nothing bad will happen to Ettie as long as you do exactly what I say."

"Which is?" *Please, please don't hurt my baby, please...*

"Turn the car around. Get Greg to drive you back to Kirke's house."

"How the hell...?"

"Your pepper spray, Mommy. A listening device, state-of-the art. Much like the grills in my backyard. Like Kirke said, don't ever eat the mushrooms."

He'd heard *everything*. Nan glanced at Greg and lowered her voice. "What do you want?"

"You. Dead. Once that happens, Ettie will be returned to her father unharmed."

"Why?"

Ted laughed. "I think Kirke explained it best. You don't get to take Stone away from me."

Nan couldn't speak. It was true. "You killed Beulah."

"Yes. And Willa and Ruthie and my dad, and of course, sweet little irritating-as-all-hell Janie. Little brat." She heard a kissing sound. "I have to say, I think Ettie is a far sweeter kid. Stone and I will raise her as our own."

God, this was so twisted, and she had no clue what to do. "Why Kirke's house?"

"Because I'm on my way there now, or should I say, we are on our way. And don't even think of contacting Stone, Nanouk, because I have your daughter's life in my hands, and to be honest, I wouldn't think twice."

"What about Greg?"

"Send him away. He'll object, but you must insist."

"He won't buy it."

"He'd better or he'll have a bullet in his head. Again, don't even think of warning him. I'll be listening... and watching."

Nan's eyes darted around the front of the car looking for a camera. She heard Ted laugh. "You'll never find it, beautiful." She heard car horns on the other end—Ted was driving. "I have to go. Be there."

Nan slowly lowered her phone and closed her eyes. She didn't have a choice if she was to save Ettie.

MILES KIRKE FROWNED as her car drove back up his driveway. What the hell was going on? He called out to his bodyguard, but no answer came. Instead, he heard the wail of a baby and rocked back. What the hell?

He stalked back into the house and followed the sound of the baby's cries. In his study, he saw the child laying on the couch. "What the fuck is going on?" He moved toward the child, but then an arm was hooked around his neck. An arm with a knife.

"Hi, Miles," Ted Vanderberg said cheerfully. "Man, have you

been spilling the tea? To make up for it, I'm going to need you to do something."

Miles, feeling the steel of the knife against the skin of his neck, swallowed hard. "And what's that?"

"I'm going to need you to shoot and kill Nan Songbird."

As EXPECTED, Greg did not want to be sent away, but Nan told him. "Miles has a fortress there. I just need a few more hours to talk to him. Please, *Gregory*, I'm sure Stone needs you back at base." She tried to communicate her fear with her eyes, but it was difficult since she was aware she was being watched. *Jesus, Ettie, I'm coming...*

Greg stared at her, and eventually he threw up his hands. "Mr Vanderberg told me to do whatever you wanted, so I guess..." He sighed. "I'll be back to pick you up in two hours... Nan."

He never called her that. Ever. It was always *Ms. Songbird*, or *Ma'am*. It gave her hope he knew something was up.

Her legs shaking, she got out of the car and walked up the stone steps. She heard Greg drive off down the driveway. No one came to meet her, and she guessed Ted was already inside— waiting to kill her.

Oh God, Stone, I'm sorry. I'm sorry, I love you...

CHAPTER TWENTY-TWO

Stone knew something was wrong, but he couldn't figure out what. It was something deep down in his bones—the fact that he wasn't with either Nan or Ettie—that he couldn't lay eyes on them instantly made him nervous.

Ted had offered to take Ettie out for a drive; she couldn't settle down without her mom near today. She was fractious and wriggly and even being in Stone's arms couldn't make her happy. She wanted Nan.

Stone's mother had smiled after Ted left with Ettie. "You were like that sometimes, only wanted your mommy." She grinned at her son. "Don't worry, I won't tell anyone. Janie was the same."

"Not Ted?"

A cloud passed over his mother's face. "No. He only ever wanted to be near *you*, Stone. Maybe a little too much."

Stone frowned. "Too much?"

His mother sighed. "Sometimes I would catch him at night. He would sit on the edge of your bed. Sometimes he would even snuggle up to you. It was a little odd. Went beyond hero worship." She waved her hand. "Ah listen to me, penny psychologist. You were just his world for a long time. He still worships you."

"*Ted*?" Stone was incredulous. "Really?"

"You haven't noticed?"

Stone's mind traveled back, and now he thought about it, he could see a pattern. Diana was watching him. "He's always been a little jealous of anyone you're close to; that's why he's not as friendly with your friends and lovers at first. He soon gets over it. Look at Eli. Would he manage him if he hated him?"

Something like unease was creeping into Stone's mind. "Ted was jealous. Of Eli? Of... Nan?"

"I think he got over it," Diana was tidying up now. "He likes Nan a lot and he adores Ettie."

Stone's cell phone rang. Greg. "Mr. Vanderberg, I'm currently at Miles Kirke's place—Ms. Songbird asked me to bring her here this morning. I'm sorry—she asked me not to tell you. Something's wrong. We left about twenty minutes ago, but almost immediately she asked me turn around. She'd taken a phone call, and I don't think it was a friendly one. And," Greg sighed, "she called me *Gregory*. Mr. Vanderberg, I think she was trying to tell me something. Ms. Songbird knows my full name is Gregson."

"Miles Kirke?" Stone was astonished. "Okay, I'm on my way. Send me the GPS."

"Will do. Look, I'm going back in, even if nothing's happening, and Ms. Songbird is okay. I'll risk her wrath."

"Do it. Nothing happens to her, understood? Do what you have to. I'm on my way."

Diane was looking at him, concern on her face. "What was that?"

Stone turned to her. "Nan is in trouble... I think Miles Kirke has something to do with Beulah's murder."

. . .

THE FIRST THING Nan saw was her daughter, oblivious, gurgling happily on the couch. She darted toward her.

"Uh-uh." Nan froze and turned. Ted, grinning, was standing behind a seated Miles, who was taped to the chair, a knife to his throat. Miles was aiming at gun directly at her.

"Well, hello, beautiful."

Nan felt no fear for herself, only for her daughter. "Don't do this, Ted."

Ted rolled his eyes. "Oh, come on, you think I went to all this trouble *not* to kill you?"

"You won't get away with it. Stone will know, and he will destroy you, especially if you kill Ettie."

"I have no intention of killing your daughter... unless you make this difficult for me."

Nan met Miles' terrified gaze and knew the man knew, as she did, that Ted was lying. She steeled herself. "Then do it. Get your lackey to shoot me."

Ted smiled. "You're right." He pressed the blade to Mile's neck. "Put a bullet in her belly, please, Mr. Kirke."

Nan's hands clenched as Miles aimed at her. She met his gaze again. He smiled and opened his mouth to speak.

"Run," he said and turned the gun on himself, shooting through his chest and hitting Ted as the bullet smashed through them both. Ted screamed out in pain as the bullet hit him in the left side of his abdomen and he crumpled just as Miles' head dropped and blood began streaming from his mouth.

Nan reacted immediately, diving toward Ettie and grabbing her up. She ran from the room and yanked open the front door, out into the open air. For a split second she hesitated, not knowing where to go. Should she go out onto the road, hope a passing car would pick her up?

She heard a roar behind her. No, Ted would expect that. Instead she took off, running into the woods, diving around the thickly knotted trees. She heard a bullet ping off a nearby tree, and her adrenaline surged. He would kill them both if he caught up with them.

She held her daughter tight to her chest as she ran, zig-zagging through the trees. It was a mistake to come in here, she thought, as the undergrowth became ever denser, and her legs kept getting caught up.

She didn't even see the branch that took her down, buried under a mess of tangled twigs. Her foot hooked around it and she fell, twisting desperately so she wouldn't land on Ettie. Ettie started to cry.

"Shh, baby, Shh..." But it was too late. Her ankle had snapped, and Nan felt sick with the pain of it. Her vision clouded with pain. It was over. She heard Ted approach and hurriedly yanked out her cell phone. She was determined Ted would not get away with killing her and Ettie. She teed up a message to Stone, and as Ted burst through the undergrowth, his gun aiming directly at her, she snapped the photo and sent it.

"Fucking bitch." He aimed the gun at her belly and shot her. Nan jerked with the agony of it.

"Don't hurt Ettie, please... do what you want to me, but don't hurt her."

"Fuck you, bitch, you shouldn't have run." He had just aimed the gun at Ettie when from the side, a huge black-suited man dived into him and tackled him to the ground, pounding his face and breaking the arm that held the gun.

Nan, light-headed from blood loss, crawled to her baby and wrapped her in her arms. If she was going to die, she wanted to be holding her precious Ettie. She pressed her lips to Ettie's tiny head. "I love you so much, Tee-Tee, so much. Promise you'll look after your daddy for me."

She drifted in and out of consciousness as Greg picked her up and carried them both out of the woods. The last thing she heard was Stone's voice screaming her name, and the sound of a helicopter landing before she gave in to the darkness.

CHAPTER TWENTY-THREE

Stone held Ettie in his arms as they all waited in the relative's room for news on Nan. Stone, like his mother, was still reeling from the news that Ted had been behind everything. Ted was in custody now, admitting everything in the hope of a plea deal, but the assistant DA, standing in for the critically injured Miles Kirke, wasn't having any of it. Ted was being charged with the murders of Joseph Vanderberg, Willa Green, Ruthie Price, and Beulah Tegan, as well as the attempted murders of Nan Songbird, Ettie Songbird, and Miles Kirke. Ted would go away for a very, very long time—and worse for him, he would never see his beloved Stone again.

Diana Vanderberg was rallying, but she was also shattered. "Why didn't I see it?"

They had found Miles' file about Ted in his home, and Diana and Stone had to come to terms with the fact that Ted had murdered Janie, and his father had covered it up. The twin betrayals and the horrendous damage Ted had left in his wake was too much to process, and they both just concentrated on caring for Ettie and waiting for news on Nan.

A few hours after she had been taken into surgery, the doctor came to find them. "She's weak, but she's a trooper. There's a long way to go, but she should be fine."

The relief was overwhelming. "Can we see her?" Stone was desperate to be with her.

"She's in recovery, but yes, in about an hour." He smiled and nodded at Ettie, asleep in her father's arms. "She's precious."

"They both are," Stone's voice was choked, and he pressed his lips to his daughter's head. "God help me, *they both are...*"

AN HOUR LATER, he was allowed in to see Nan. She was groggy but smiled when she saw him and Ettie. "Hey you."

Stone bent his head to kiss her. "Thank God, Nan. Thank God."

She chuckled. "It would have taken more than a bullet to take me away from you."

He leaned his forehead against hers. "I love you so much, Nanouk Songbird."

"As I love you, Stoney."

He chuckled. "Stoney?"

"Seems to me you're my Stoney."

"I am. Always yours."

Nan smiled and reached for Ettie. Stone handed her over and sat on the edge of the bed. "Are you in pain?"

"A little but they gave me morphine. I kind of wish they hadn't, because now I can't feed Ettie myself."

Stone stroked Nan's hair back from her face. "I think after everything, that's a small sacrifice."

"I'll miss it, is all."

"Listen, we have all the time in the world to bond with Ettie now. At our own pace, in our own home. What say we try to find somewhere on Oyster Bay, a place where she can play outside, and we can get a couple of dogs."

Nan smiled. "Not too..."

"*Palatial*. I know. Look, with all this crap about Ted, the Vanderberg name is pretty much in the toilet. The papers are having a field day."

"I'm sorry, baby."

Stone shook his head. "Don't you dare apologize, Nanouk—for anything. You nearly died because of me."

"It was *not* because of you," she said forcefully, then winced. "Sorry, painful twinge. But Stoney, my life began when I met you and the day I became pregnant with Tee-Tee. I mean... I'm the luckiest girl in the world."

"Only you would be that optimistic after just having a bullet removed from your body," Stone said fondly, "What I'm saying is... when we get married, I'm taking yours and Ettie's last name."

Nan's eyes widened. "You are? What does your mom think about that?"

"She's supportive. Besides, it's too beautiful a name for you and Ettie, and it's the freakin' twenty-first century. So, yes, if you'll let me, I'll be Mr. Stone Songbird."

Nan had tears in her eyes. "I can't wait to be your wife, Stoney."

Stone smiled. "Marry me, Nan. As soon as you get out of here, marry me."

And Nan knew that from now on, her life would be happy, fun, and full of love...

The End.

SIGN UP TO RECEIVE FREE BOOKS

Sign Up to Receive Free E-Books and Audiobook Codes.

Would you like to read **The Unexpected Nanny, Dirty Little Virgin** and **other romance books** **for free?**

You can sign up to receive these free e-books and audiobooks by typing this link into your browser:

https://www.steamyromance.info/free-books-and-audiobooks-hot-and-steamy/

Or this one:

https://www.steamyromance.info/the-unexpected-nanny-free/

PREVIEW OF ROCKSTAR UNTAMED
A SINGLE DAD VIRGIN ROMANCE

By Michelle Love

Blurb

Rockstar Bodhi Creed is blindsided when his ex-girlfriend, Gemma, turns up with a six-year-old son, Tim, and tells Bodhi that it's his turn to play house with his son. Completely out of his depth, he none-the-less tries his best to juggle his superstar career with his paternal duties, but his son is reluctant to bond with him.

Sailor King is working as an assistant to a Hollywood agent, Maurice Winston, unhappily. Her boss is a leach and a creep, and the day he gropes her, she retaliates by slapping him. To her horror, the incident is witnessed by the incredulous Bodhi, who, to her surprise, backs her up and fires Maurice as his agent.

Maurice vows to destroy Bodhi's career and tells Sailor she'll never work in Hollywood again. She shoots back that that would suit her fine. Bodhi tells them both Sailor has already got herself hired by him.

Sailor starts her new job as Bodhi's assistant, but soon gravitates to caring for Tim, with whom she finds common ground. Both were the product of a one-night stand and both lead confusing childhoods. But Sailor hides a bigger secret; less than a year ago, she escaped from a cult in which she had been raised and still carries the scars of that experience with her. She is still freaked out by the concept of freedom, but also chaffs against any kind of control. Looking after Tim gives her a sense of stability and under her care, the boy starts to thrive.

Bodhi, whose reputation as a man-whore is well-known, is grateful to the young woman and is drawn to her, but Sailor keeps him at a distance. He doesn't blame her, he revels in his promiscuity, but he also makes the decision to spend more time with Tim, and by extension, Sailor. Soon, the two of them begin to be more than friends and when their relationship goes to the next level; Sailor confides her past to him as well as one more surprising revelation: she is a virgin.

PART ONE

Chicago, Illinois

January

Bodhi Creed breathed in the scent of the crowd; sweat, excitement, almost frenzied adoration. He stood at the front of the stage, taking in the love of his fans as he finished his song, putting everything into the final few chords. His voice soaring and dipping with perfect pitch. He knew he could make people shiver with the sound of his voice. He finished the song and took his final bow, taking his time to wave to the crowd as he left the stage, his whole system flooding with adrenaline. Who needed drugs when performing could make you feel like this? He grinned to his crew and his band as he walked back to his dressing room, thanking each of them personally.

There was a reason people loved Bodhi Creed. It wasn't just that he had pulled himself out of a hellish path from a drug-fueled death during his early career or that his face could sell anything as much as his singing voice. It was that he was genuinely a humble man, offstage and on. He had his demons, what rock god didn't? But now, nearing forty, he still appealed to fans of all ages.

Bodhi walked back to his dressing room, pushed the door open and almost choked. Poppy, his personal assistant of two months, had been 'cleansing' his space again, burning sage and wafting it around the windowless room. She grinned at him. "Hey, boss."

She had bright pink hair, tattoos up and down her arms, and wore clothes that would make a fetishist blush. She looked like a real rock goddess, Bodhi smiled fondly at her more than he ever did.

God, he was tired. This had been the last date of the tour that had lasted well over a year, and he was exhausted, drained, ready for some down time. Bodhi knew himself, it was times like these he would have, back in the day, reached for the bottle or the white stuff. The thought of cocaine now made him feel sick. Jimi Hendrix, Layne Staley, Scott Weiland, Shannon Hoon, he used their names as a mantra to stay away from drugs now, even when he was depressed.

Now as he ran his hand through his dark curls and slumped down onto the sofa, a cold soda in hand, he looked for respite in other ways. His good friend, Claudio Fonseca, an artist, had invited him to go stay at his farmhouse in the Tuscan hills for the summer, picking olives and chilling out. Bodhi couldn't wait. Two months of Italian sun, wine, food and relaxation in the company of good friends. He could see his mom at her home in Florence. Bodhi longed to go back to Italy. His American father had brought the family over to America just after Bodhi had been born, and growing up in Seattle, Bodhi had longed to know the place he had come from. When his dad died, his mom sold her house and went back, begging Bodhi to go with her. But by then, he was a star, and he needed to be in Los Angeles for his career.

He looked up as the door opened and Franklin, the theater manager, stuck his head in.

"Sorry to interrupt, Bodhi, but there's a kid out here to see you."

Bodhi was surprised. A kid? Usually, his groupies were nubile young women. "Show them in, please. Thanks, Frank." He always, always took the time to talk with his fans, despite how tired he was, without them, he was nothing.

A kid with dark curls, not older than ten, pushed shyly into the room, and Bodhi got up to greet him. "Hey there, what's your name, kiddo?"

The kid blinked his huge green eyes up at Bodhi, seeming dumbstruck. Bodhi didn't see the woman who had entered behind the child until she spoke softly.

"His name is Tim, Bodhi."

Bodhi, recognizing the voice immediately, looked up, and a shock ran through him.

"Gemma?"

The blonde woman smiled at him. "Been a long time, hasn't it?"

Bodhi stared at her, still stunned to see his former lover. She was Bodhi's senior by five years, had not dulled her beauty, but there was a haunted, desperate look in her eyes.

"Must be about ten yea…" Bodhi broke off, realization dawning, and he gazed down at the young boy standing between them. Dark hair, bright green eyes. Bodhi's eyes. There really was no question.

Gemma looked at him, her eyes filling with tears as she watched him put the pieces together. "I'm sorry to do this to you, Bodhi…I really am. But I'm not doing so well. I need to go away for a while, alone. And I thought it's time. It's time for Tim to know his daddy."

Bodhi's whole body felt as if he'd been hit by a sledgehammer as he gazed down into the face of his son.

Miami, Florida

SAILOR KING FOLLOWED her minder through the mall. It was cool, almost chilly, inside the spacious building, but Sailor didn't mind. Even January in Florida was too hot for her. Her dark hair stuck to her forehead and to the back of her neck. Monica, her minder, gave her an annoyed look.

"What's wrong with you today? You know Bartholomew will punish me if we're more than two hours. We haven't even found your wedding dress yet."

Sailor stared back at Monica blankly. She felt so tired lately, so hopeless that she had stopped taking the anti-depressant tablets they had given her all her life, and now she felt as if her brain would go mad. She didn't want this, didn't want to be married to a man more than twice her age. She knew within the ranks of the organization that she was 'lucky.' Other girls were clamoring to be partnered with Bart Foy, their leader, their captain.

But Bart had chosen her. She had known the unease of his lascivious gaze on her body; her curves, her flat belly, her full breasts since she was a teenager. He had held her face in his hands when she was just fourteen, an entire decade ago. It had been decreed, she would be his new wife when she reached the age of womanhood, in their ideology, it would be her twenty-fifth birthday, which was in a few weeks.

Bart Foy had been married twice before. His first wife was Tamsin, about whom nobody knew much. They had been married before Bart formed the 'Children of Love' commune, deep in the Florida Everglades. His wife had left him after refusing to join him in his 'mission.' Bart's second wife, Clotilde, was a beautiful, loving, Frenchwoman with dark brown hair tumbling down her back and a sweet nature. She had joined the group as a teacher for the children and Sailor had been one of her wards. She had been particularly close to Clotilde, Tilly to those who loved her, and when, one shocking, horrific night, Tilly had been found dead, Sailor had been devastated.

Bart made them all walk past Tilly's body, laid out on the shrine in their temple. "I want you to look, children. Look what sin can bring."

Sailor had always wondered what he meant. When she found out, from hushed whispers in the schoolyard, that Tilly had been having an affair with another man, and that she had been stabbed to death, at around eleven, Sailor knew what that meant.

The terror when Bart had chosen her for his next wife had been all-encompassing, but she had buried her head in the sand, thinking the day would never come. Then three months ago, he had summoned her.

"My dearest Sailor, your womanhood is fast approaching, and to me, it seems the perfect time for us to become one. Your birthday will serve as our wedding day, do you understand?"

She nodded, the fear inside overwhelming her ability to speak. Bart smiled and touched her cheek. "Good. Now, I'm afraid we have to deal with a little unpleasantness before you go. As you know, I take my role here very seriously, and in choosing you as my wife, I need you to be an ambassador for us all." He paused, studying her. "You were very close to Clotilde, I know. She betrayed all of us, Sailor. All of us. Her punishment...well..."

He picked up a folder and handed it to her. "I'm going to leave you alone here for a few minutes to study what's in that folder. When I return, this matter will be closed. This is what happens when my women betray me, Sailor, understand? That's the only reason why I'm showing you these photographs."

Sailor nodded again. "Good girl. I'll leave you alone."

He left his office and Sailor heard the lock being clicked from outside. She opened the folder, feeling nausea rise up in her, and a small moan of despair escaped her as she looked at the first photograph. Tilly looked terrified as the two men in the picture held her down, obviously making sure the photographer got a good shot of her. The next photograph made Sailor cry out. The knife was buried deep in Tilly's stomach, and her face was contorted in agony. Sailor was trembling as she looked through every photograph of Tilly's murder, each one more stark and brutal than the last. The last image broke Sailor and she whimpered in despair. There was another man now, strapped down to a chair, gagged and bound, his face contorted with grief as he gazed down at his dead sweetheart's body. Tilly's lover. They'd made him watch while they killed her. Sailor started to cry. Bart's meaning was obvious. Step out of line and you die.

It was at that moment that Sailor knew she had to risk everything and escape the only life she had ever known.

Monica was chatting with the saleswoman in the wedding shop. She was used to Monica and Sailor coming now, Sailor had deliberately been picky over her choice, giving herself time to check out the fitting rooms, and any potential escape routes. She'd nearly been foiled by Monica insisting on accompanying her to the fitting rooms. Sailor had used her only weapon, she was Bart's chosen one. "I don't think," she'd told Monica knowingly, "that Bart would be too pleased that you laid eyes on my body before the wedding. I am his, Monica, and his alone."

Her implied threat hit the mark, and Monica let her change alone. Sailor was careful, never taking too long between changes to reappear but still, she managed to figure out the layout of the store.

Now, she could barely wait. Careful. Careful. She took her time choosing then took the dress with her. It was a huge, completely inappropriate choice, layers and layers of tulle that she would never wear in a million years, but Sailor knew what she was doing. The shirt she was wearing today was too big, plaid and her combat pants. In the many pockets, she had stashed the money she had been saving for the last three months, squirreled away and stolen from the commune's money cache, a little at a time. Her birth certificate, with only her mother identified on it, and social security number, and any other thing she found in Bart's office that terrible day, that she could use. She even had a small penknife, tucked in the back pocket of her pants. In all, she only had a couple of hundred dollars, but it was enough for a bus ticket. After that, she'd figure something out.

Monica didn't even blink as Sailor walked toward the fitting rooms, calling back to her, "I won't be a sec."

MONICA SMIRKED. That atrocity that Sailor was carrying would take more than a 'sec' to change into. Stupid little whore. Lording it over her like she was some special kind of shit. Look how that worked out for Tilly, bitch. She turned back to the saleswoman, who knew all about the commune, all about Bart's proclivities. Monica had told her all about them one night in bed. The girl, Bettina, had been a good, inexperienced, lay and Monica wouldn't mind another go around.

The alarm started screeching through the shop, and both women said. "What the fuck?"

"The fire escape door," Bettina looked terrified as Monica

cursed loudly and drew out a blade, darting towards the fitting rooms.

"Fucking bitch..." She saw the fire escape door standing wide open, and the wedding dress dumped in the doorway. "Fucking whore bitch cunt!" Monica screamed, racing down the corridor and around the corner towards the exit, Bettina close behind her. They both trod on the dress in their eagerness to get out, but Sailor had ripped the tulle to shreds, and their feet got caught, tangled, and they both fell. Bettina shrieked as Monica's knife came way too close to her neck.

"Shut up, you stupid bitch," Monica sliced away at the fabric, trying to free them. Out of the fire escape, they could see the parking lot, and Monica raked it with her eyes, trying to spot Sailor.

SAILOR DROPPED from the top of the fitting room wall and slid silently into the main room. Inspiration striking, she went to the register, hoping against hope that some rich musketry-muck had paid with cash. She was in luck. She scooped a wad of twenties out of the register, raking every note and coin in there into her pocket. Listening intently to make sure she could still hear Monica cursing away in the back, she quickly took stock and grabbed the wigs from the mannequins in the window. In a high-end store like this, they used real human hair wigs, and she could use them to disguise herself and then sell them. She stuffed them all into a plastic bag and then she was free. Running to the exit of the mall and out into the Florida sunshine, she flagged down a cab and asked the driver to take her to the bus station. In a half-hour, she was on the bus, hunched down, hiding...

And breathing freely for the first time in her young life.

Los Angeles

Six months later...

BODHI ATE a piece of toast half-heartedly as he watched his son push his cereal around his bowl. "Kiddo, that will get all mushy if you do that."

"I like it mushy."

Bodhi sighed. Well, at least Tim was speaking to him now. "Okay, then."

Tim glanced at his father briefly, then looked away when Bodhi met his gaze. "Can I go to school now?"

Bodhi nodded, not knowing what else to do. Since, Gemma had left Tim with him, this had been their routine. Tim, thankfully, had settled into his new school happily, but at home...

At home, Bodhi thought, bitterly, it's been a Cold War. Tim hadn't taken to him at all. He was rude, silent, and resentful. Bodhi knew Tim blamed him for his mother leaving him, but Bodhi had no idea what else to do. Poppy, his assistant, had suddenly quit, telling him she was sorry but looking after a kid hadn't been in the job description.

"It's just not my jam, Bodhi, I'm sorry."

Since then, Tim had seen off two childminders and one English tutor. Bodhi had canceled gigs, interviews, recording sessions to try and bond with his son, but nothing was working. Tim was vastly unimpressed with his father's musical friends, couldn't care less about the instruments Bodhi played. Even the priceless grand piano in the living room held no interest. Tim kept to his room, his vast-well-stocked-with-everything-a-boy-could-need room, and didn't even explore the pool or the grounds of Bodhi's luxurious Hollywood Hills mansion.

Bodhi got into the driver's seat of his RAV4 and they began another silent drive to Tim's school. Gemma had insisted that

Tim had the best education and Bodhi, ignoring the fact she was making demands while asking an enormous favor, agreed. God, he would do anything for his son. He knew that the moment Gemma had brought Tim into his life. He just wished he could feel like anything but a deadbeat dad.

, "Hey, kiddo? What say we go shopping for a new laptop for you this weekend?"

Tim looked at him with those huge green eyes even wider. "Really?"

"Really."

"Thank you, Bodhi."

Progress, although he wished Tim would call him Dad. Deciding not to push it and ruin the moment, he just smiled at Tim and was rewarded by a slight smile. "That one you have is ancient; I'm surprised you can still use it."

Tim's smile disappeared, and he looked away from his father. "Evan brought me that laptop before he went away."

Ah, the sainted Evan. Bodhi sighed. When Tim talked at all about his life before Bodhi, it was about his former stepfather Evan. Evan Teal was a detective up in Portland, and to hear Tim talk, the most amazing man he'd ever met. Evan had practically raised Tim from birth so Bodhi couldn't help, but be grateful. He just wished and hoped that Teal had some faults, so that he wouldn't feel such like a loser. When Evan and Gemma had split up, Tim had been devastated. And now Bodhi had insulted Evan's final gift to Tim.

Bodhi opened his mouth to apologize but closed it again. Why bother? He dropped Tim off at school, barely receiving a "Bye."

He checked his watch and drove into the center of L.A. to his agent's office. Maurice had summoned him, obviously trying to get him back in the game after six months away. Bodhi's little sabbatical wasn't making Maurice his fifteen percent, and he was getting antsy about it.

Maybe it is time I got back to work, Bodhi thought now as he steered his way into a parking space. I'm sure not doing anything helpful at home. He sighed and got out of the car, and opened the office door.

S<small>AILOR GRITTED HER TEETH</small>, for the fourth time that morning, Maurice Winston leaned across her, pressing his sweaty body against hers. "I'll move," she said disdainfully, pushing back her chair, so it rammed him in the ankle.

She had worked for Maurice for three months, and if she hadn't been desperate for money, and eager to hide out in her little apartment, she would have quit the day after she started.

Maurice Winston was a leach, a man who clearly saw his assistant as his property. When he wasn't making gross suggestions to her, he was outright rude, criticizing her at every turn, even though Sailor ran his office like a tight ship. Her past, the rules, the chores of the commune had left her with one good thing; she was organized, efficient, punctual and she knew Maurice knew it too.

But the harassment he gave her every day, was it worth it? She had been searching out other job opportunities, but it seemed the rest of L.A. wasn't hiring just yet. She had no choice to put up with his behavior.

Escaping the clutches of the 'Children of Love' had only been the start of her tumultuous new life. Getting off the bus in L.A. after traveling for days, she had checked herself into a small motel and after a hot shower, a night's sleep and vending machine food, she had taken stock. The money she had stolen was enough that she could manage for a month or so. She had no remorse about taking it, either. She checked the Miami local news on a computer at the local library. The robbery and her disappearance were never mentioned. *No, because I know too much, hey, Bart? I know about Tilly. What you did to her.*

Even now, the thought of Bart's anger scared her. She knew he would try to find her and if he did, she was a dead woman. She had constant nightmares about him stabbing her to death. But as time went on, she began to relax into her new life. She found a studio flat close to Maurice's office, and although it was tiny, she loved it. She began to make it her own with books, records, and flowers on every surface. She even loved the small kitchen and began to teach herself how to cook. After work each night, she would come home, change out of her work clothes into sweats and eat, watch TV, play music or read. And she loved every moment. It was hers and hers alone.

MAURICE WAS READING A LETTER, oblivious to Sailor's annoyance. She sat back down in her chair and started to go through emails, occasionally mentioning important notes to him. He grunted as if he wasn't listening properly and Sailor rolled her eyes. It would mean her staying late and making a cheat sheet of everything he needed to know. *Asshole.*

She was so engrossed in her work that she failed to notice he had put down the letter and was standing too close behind her. Sailor stood to go grab a photocopy and Maurice pounced.

He swept a foot under hers and Sailor lost balance, falling into Maurice's clutches. He tumbled her to the couch and began to kiss her. Sailor struggled, panicking, angry and terrified. "Get the fuck off me!"

Maurice grinned. "Come on now, Sailor, you know this has been coming for a while. Don't fight it. I know you want me."

Sailor pounded his chests with her fists. "Let me go, cocksucker! Get off me!"

Maurice, still grinning, pushed her skirt up to her hips. "Come on, lovely girl, show me that sweet cunt of yours."

Sailor lost it then, and drawing back her arm, she punched Maurice in the eye, her ring tearing a piece of flesh from below his eyebrow. He rocked back, roaring in pain. "Fucking bitch!"

Sailor scrambled away from him, but he grabbed her ankle and pulled her back. "I'll fucking kill you, you little whore."

"Join the fucking queue, asshole," Sailor hissed and rammed her foot into his groin, hard. Maurice screamed and doubled over, and Sailor skittered away from him. "I quit, you monster. And believe me, I'm going to the police and the press. You don't ever get to put your hands on me again, motherfucker!" She was raging now, every ounce of hurt in her life coming back to her, and releasing through her anger and hurt. "Who the fuck, do you think you are touching me like that?"

Maurice smiled nastily. "More than you'll ever be in this town, cunt. How are you this naïve? Did you really think I hired you for your typing skills? No, Princess, it was because I wanted to fuck you and I always get what I want."

He lunged for her again and got his hands around her throat, choking her as she tried to scream, struggling to pull his hands away. Maurice kicked her legs apart and tore her panties from her, and then she heard his belt loosen, his fly open.

Oh god, no, please, not like this...

She twisted away from him, and his hands loosened enough for her to scream at the top of her lungs. Maurice's body weight was heavy on her, and she knew that he had the upper hand.

and shock, hauled Maurice off her and threw him across the room. Maurice was short, the other was a giant, and Maurice was no match.

"What the fuck, do you think you're doing?" He roared at Maurice who was trying to stand up. Her savior held out his hands to Sailor and, gratefully, she took them, her whole body trembling. "Are you okay, sweetheart?"

Sailor gazed into the man's huge green eyes, seeing only empathy, and she shook her head. He put his arm gently around her shoulders. "It's okay, lovely, I won't let him near you again. You...," he turned back to Maurice. "You're so fucking fired, Maurice. How dare you behave like this?"

Maurice was straightening up his clothes. "Oh, fuck off, Bodhi, it was just a little fun."

Bodhi's face was a picture of utter disgust and rage. "A little fun? Fun? When a woman is screaming like that, that's not fun, Maurice, that's rape." He turned his beautiful eyes back to Sailor. "Honey, what's your name?"

"Sailor." A whisper, her throat raw from being choked. Bodhi swept a gentle hand over her cheek, brushing away her tears.

"Sailor, sweetheart, we need to go to the police. I'll back you one hundred percent."

"Now wait a minute..."

"Shut the fuck up, Maurice. Now." A lion's roar.

Maurice shut the fuck up. Bodhi steered Sailor into a chair and pulled out his phone, but Sailor put her hand over it and shook her head. Bodhi frowned. "Are you sure?"

She nodded, meeting his gaze. Even through her teary eyes, her shock was slowly turning to numbness, she was enthralled with this man's beauty, his grace, his kindness. She wanted to close her eyes and lean into him and sleep with his arms around her. She sighed. "I just want to go," she said softly.

Bodhi touched her cheek. "Then we'll go. Maurice, you're a lucky man that Sailor doesn't want to press charges, but as from this moment, you are no longer my agent."

Maurice seemed to realize that his biggest cash cow was on the way out of the door. "Now, wait, Bodhi, there's no need..."

Bodhi turned his furious eyes on the other man. "There is every need, asshole."

Maurice smiled nastily. "Then you should know, I'll do everything in my power to finish you in this town. Everything."

"Go right ahead," Bodhi said calmly. "Try it. See how far you'll get." He took Sailor's hand and pulled her to her feet. "Come on, sweetie, get your things and we'll get out of here."

Sailor nodded and quickly grabbed her purse and a few personal items from her desk. Maurice watched her.

"I don't even need to tell you that you'll never work in this town again, you little bitch."

Bodhi stepped up to Maurice and punched him across the room. "You don't ever talk to her or any other woman like that again, motherfucker. You're lucky Sailor doesn't want the police involved, but believe me, I hear of anything else like this, and I'll call your wife and her billionaire daddy. And by the way, if a check for three, no, six, six months severance pay for Sailor isn't in the mail by tomorrow, I will go the police. So, go fuck yourself." He looked at Sailor, watching him, waiting by the door and he smiled the most beautiful smile at her. Sailor felt her stomach flutter. "Besides," Bodhi continued, "you're so wrong. Sailor already has another job. If she agrees, she'll be working for me and twice at the salary. Not only that, but I will make sure every employer in town knows and respects her. Think about that, Maurice."

He stalked over to Sailor and offered her his hand. "Ready to go, lovely?"

Sailor smiled and took his hand.

IN BODHI'S CAR, Sailor finally stopped her hands trembling. She looked at the man beside her. Bodhi Creed, she'd heard of him, of course, he was her boss's, scratch that, ex-boss's – biggest client and yet she hadn't met or even spoken to him before today. His magnetism was a powerful thing, even just sitting beside him, she couldn't help wonder at his incredible physical beauty. Swarthy skin, stubble, dark curls flopping around his head. And those eyes, god, she could get lost in them. She pulled herself up sharply. Do not get a crush.

"Thank you for what you did back there, Mr. Creed. I can never repay you."

He turned and smiled at her. "It's Bodhi, and there's nothing to repay. Are you feeling okay now?"

She nodded. "I am, thank you. Where are we going?"

Bodhi blinked. "I was just heading home. Automatic, you know? Would you feel more comfortable going somewhere public? I thought I would make you some lunch."

A rock god making her lunch? Was this happening? He was so…normal. So, down to earth. "You really don't have to."

Bodhi grinned. "Full disclosure. I like making food for people, I enjoy the company. How about if I ask instead of assuming? Sailor, would you like to have lunch with me?"

And Sailor knew without a doubt that she most definitely would.

Sailor groaned and put her hand on her belly. Bodhi Creed knew how to cook. "I think you may have killed me." She grinned at him. "That was incredible, thank you. I won't need to eat for a few…weeks, I think."

Bodhi laughed, spearing the last piece of his steak into his mouth. A blue cheese and steak salad was his specialty. Throw in freshly baked bread, that he admitted he'd got from the store, fresh, plump peaches and a light Pinot Grigio. Sailor was in heaven. "Sure I can't tempt you with some gelato or anything?"

"God," Sailor said, "I love gelato, but even my pudding stomach is full."

"Your pudding stomach?" Bodhi laughed loudly, and Sailor grinned at him.

"Yeah, you know, when you're so full of savory stuff, but then someone offers you sugar and all bets are off?"

"Except today. Pudding stomach is out of action?"

"Yes, sir."

Bodhi chuckled. "If my mom was here, you'd been talked into it. She's been making gelato since I was a kid, before that even. Family recipe."

"Your mom's Italian?"

"She is. An artist. She lives in Florence, and I don't get to see her as often as I would like. She would like you, Sailor. She hates women who pick at their food. So, do I. One of life's great pleasures, food."

"Especially if it's made by a rockstar," Sailor grinned and, laughing, he toasted her with his glass.

They were sitting out on his patio, looking over the hills at Los Angeles in the distance. His huge infinity pool shone bright blue and a small breeze took some of the afternoon heat off. Sailor studied her host. "Do you live here alone?"

Bodhi shook his head. "No, my son is here with me at the moment. He's ten, well, only just. His name is Tim."

He reached into his pocket for his wallet, then pulled out a photograph to show Sailor. She studied it. "Adorable. He is your twin," she said, nodding.

"In looks only, I'm afraid," Bodhi smiled a little sadly. "While his old Pa is an exhibitionist and a show-off, Tim is definitely erring on the side of science. Not that it's a bad thing. He could run rings around me, and frequently does." Bodhi gazed out at the view for a long moment. "I didn't know him, or even that he existed until six months ago. His mother, Gemma, was my girlfriend a decade ago, but we hadn't seen or spoken for that long. She came to me, she needed some alone time and that it was my turn to raise my son." He looked at Sailor and gave a hopeless shrug. "I have no idea what I'm doing, Sailor. None. And Tim... Tim resents me."

Sailor was startled at his frankness, but touched that he opened up to her. Two hours ago, they were strangers. "I think you're probably doing better than you think, Bodhi. It has to be hard; there's no owner's manual when it comes to kids."

With a pang, she thought back to how she was raised, there, in the cult, there was definitely an owner's manual, and it was one of subjugation, terror, and manipulation.

"Sailor? You okay?"

Sailor realized she was frowning and grinned sheepishly. "Sorry. Stuck in a memory."

"Bad childhood?"

"Something like that." But she didn't want to ruin the mood by telling him anything, besides, she'd promised herself she would never tell anyone. If word got back to Bart where she was...

"I meant what I said about hiring you, Sailor. I do need a personal assistant, desperately actually. It would involve some childcare, if that doesn't freak you out, but you'd be mostly working from here with me or traveling with me."

Sailor suddenly felt shy. Being that close to this man all the time sounded like heaven. "I would work my ass off for you, Bodhi, I admit, but I wouldn't want you to think I'm taking advantage of your kindness. You've already done more for me in the few hours I've known you than anyone else in my lifetime."

Bodhi's eyes were troubled. "That's just plain wrong. Sailor, I'm just glad I was there, you don't owe me anything. But, seriously, please, give me a shot. I'll pay double, hell, triple what Winston was paying you. I know you ran interference with Winston and I when I was on sabbatical."

She started to protest, and he grinned. "Don't give me that, I know it was you. The kind emails about me taking as long as I needed, that was all you."

Sailor was bright-red now. "I know what it's like to have personal stuff going on. Sometimes, you just need to get away."

Bodhi picked up the bottle of wine and dumped the rest in her glass. "Amen to that, sister. So...yes?" He raised his glass and Sailor picked hers up.

"Yes," she said simply and tapped her glass against his.

He drove her home before he went to pick up Tim from school. "I'll pick you up tomorrow just after nine a.m.," he said, "and we'll lease you a car as soon as we can. How does that sound?"

She smiled at him. "Sounds great, thank you, Bodhi. And thank you for lunch, for the job...for saving me this morning. I hope I can repay your kindness."

Bodhi touched his finger to her cheek. "You just stay safe, little one. Maurice doesn't know where you live, does he?"

She shook her head. "No, thank god. I'll be fine. See you in the morning."

"Goodnight, Sailor."

He watched her walk up the stairs to her apartment and wave at him as she opened the door. He smiled and waved back before pulling the car back into traffic. Sailor King. When he'd opened the door to Maurice's office that morning and saw her being attacked, his anger had known no bounds. She was so tiny, so fragile, of course, his instincts had kicked in. In a way, he was relieved to be free of Maurice Winston. He'd never liked the man, but he was the best agent in Hollywood. Screw it. Why did he even need an agent? He was a musician, for crissakes. He had a contact in San Francisco, Emily Moore, who had given him her card at a concert the year before and told him to call if he needed representation. Emily was gorgeous too, but completely in love with her boyfriend, Dash Hamilton, one of the partners in the Quartet record company. Quartet had been pursuing him too, knowing his contract with Sony was almost up.

Maybe it's time for a complete change, he thought. Maybe things should slow down. It wasn't as if he didn't have enough money, just three months ago, Forbes had placed his net worth just shy of a billion dollars.

But some things were worth more than wealth, hell, a lot of things, Bodhi told himself. His son, first and foremost. He had to try and find a way to get through to Tim. Whether Tim realized it or not, Bodhi had grown to love him, it was just, at this moment, he didn't know whether he liked him.

A new life. A new assistant. A new friend. Sailor. Bodhi laughed and shook his head. How quickly life changes. Of course, he was a man, and her fragile beauty hadn't passed him by. The long waves of her dark brown hair that almost reached her waist, those big dark eyes, the pink flush of her cheeks, and her smile was breathtaking. Finally, after the trauma of her near-rape, he'd made her laugh at lunch, and her smile had made his day. It lit up her face. She was young, too young for that sort of crap to happen to her.

And she's probably too young for you, buddy, so keep your thoughts pure. With a sigh, Bodhi knew the truth of that. If he wanted to keep Sailor in his life, he would have to be professional, keep his more erotic thoughts to himself. She deserved that much from him.

At dinner, he told Tim about his new assistant, but Tim just shrugged and said "Okay." Bodhi wondered if the kid cared less about who was in his life.

"Hey, how about we go to the beach this weekend? Have you ever been to Venice Beach?"

"Evan used to take me all the time."

Of course, Bodhi was really starting to dislike this 'Evan.'

"Okay then, how about to the Caribbean? I have a friend with a place on an island down there."

Tim's eyes opened wide, and Bodhi felt a rush of joy. Finally, Tim was impressed. "For reals?"

"For reals. We can go on Friday after school, come back Sunday. What do you say?"

Tim studied his father and Bodhi, for the millionth time, wondered what was going on in his head. "Okay."

Bodhi smiled. He wanted to say more, suggest other things they could do, but he didn't want to push his luck. This was enough…for now.

"The Caribbean?" Sailor gaped at him as Bodhi laughed at her expression, the next morning.

"That's right. Want to come? All expenses paid, of course."

Sailor sat back in the passenger seat, shaking her head in disbelief. "Twenty-four hours ago, we didn't even know each other, and you saved me from being raped, or murdered, hired me at a wildly generous salary, and offered me a dream vacation to a tropical island? This isn't real."

Bodhi grinned. "Listen, if it freaks you out, just think of it as a working trip. I need to figure out what to do going forward and I need you to help me."

"On a tropical island." She repeated, then laughed. "Well… I'd love to, but I don't have a passport."

Bodhi's eyebrows shot up. "You don't?"

"Uh-ah." Sailor shook her head, her smile fading. Bodhi studied her for a long moment then turned back to the road.

"Okay…well, we could get that arranged by Friday, no problem. You have a birth certificate, right?"

Sailor nodded. She'd stolen it from Bart's cabinet the day he'd left her alone in his office, along with anything she could find with her name on. When she'd arrived in L.A., she'd gone to City Hall to legally change her name from the near unique-sounding Sailor King to the more generic Sarah Halls. At least then, she could use that name legally, but finding it hard to call herself 'Sarah,' she told people her nickname was Sailor, figuring it was safe enough to do so.

"Have you never traveled, Sailor?"

She blinked back in the present and shook her head. "No, never. Never been on a plane, never gone anywhere."

Bodhi looked amazed but then smiled. "Then it's decided. It's outrageous you've never traveled. Particularly with a name like Sailor. We'll get your passport arranged and you can come with us. Okay?"

Sailor hesitated then nodded. "Okay...thank you, Bodhi." She gave a short laugh. "I am dreaming, I'm sure."

LATER THAT DAY, after they'd spent all day talking about what Bodhi would be looking for in an assistant, and Sailor getting very excited for the challenge, she rode in the car with him as Bodhi picked Tim up from school and introduced him to Sailor. Sailor grinned at the young boy.

"Hey, it's good to meet you." She indicated a patch on his jacket of a rooster spewing fire. "Hey, you like Rhett and Link?"

Tim looked amazed that a grown-up would know who Rhett and Link were and nodded, half smiling at her. "Today we're going to eat hair gel flavored ice cream."

Sailor grinned, knowing he wanted her to give the catch-phrase of the two Internet comedians. "Let's talk about that," she quipped back, and Tim laughed delightedly.

Bodhi looked between them. "I have no idea what either of you is talking about."

Sailor rolled her eyes and winked at Tim. "Granddad," she

said in a stage whisper, making Tim giggle. Bodhi grinned at the sound, and then looked gratefully at Sailor.

"Sailor's just agreed to come to the island with us on Friday, that okay with you, buddy?"

Tim actually smiled at his father, a rare occurrence, and nodded eagerly. Bodhi held his hands up to Sailor. "See? Now you have to come."

When Tim had finally been persuaded to go to bed, Bodhi poured Sailor and himself some wine. "Girl, how the hell did you do that? He's talked more this evening than in the last six months."

He sat down, shaking his head in amazement and a little sadness and Sailor's heart went out to him. All day, she had been finding out that this megastar, this world-famous billionaire, was nothing more than a simple man at heart. His glorious face, his hard body, his rough velvet voice had made his fortune, but she could see that he craved a simpler life, one out of the spotlight. He'd shown her around his home, and she'd noticed the rooms he got most excited about were the ones where he created things, his recording studio, his workshop where he made beautiful hand-turned furniture 'to relax.' He told her about the olive groves in Tuscany where he loved to spend summers, away from public view, with his friends, his best friend Claudio, and Bodhi's artist mom. She looked through some pencil sketches, and her heart hurt when she saw the preliminary drawings he'd made of his son.

"These are gorgeous, Bodhi."

He looked pleased, giving her a shy grin. "You draw?"

She nodded. "Some. Not as good as this, and I haven't done anything for a while. Out of practice."

"You are more than welcome to come in here, use anything

you want, anytime." Bodhi leaned back against the wall, studying her. "Sailor, I've been talking about myself all day, all ego. What about you, what's your story?"

Sailor felt panicky, and she looked away from his gaze. "Not much to tell. Left a bad situation at home, come to Hollywood six months ago. Don't even know why I chose to settle here...it just seemed...far enough away."

Bodhi nodded. "Family stuff? Or boyfriend?"

Sailor chewed her lip. "Just...stuff." God, she should have figured out a story by now. It was just, in this town, people rarely cared about who you were or had been. They just needed to know if you could be useful to them. She decided to go with a potted version of the truth. "I was raised in a commune of sorts... I never knew who my father was. I was with my mom as a newborn, but she died soon after. I was alone. So, when I got older and decided the commune's rules and regulations were no longer for me, I left and came here."

Bodhi seemed satisfied with that answer. "Shame you never knew your parents. No wonder you can relate to Tim."

Sailor smiled gently. "Tim knows both his parents, they're just apart. Can I ask? Why did things with Gemma never work out?"

Bodhi sat down next to her. "Sailor, I was in my late twenties, and my career was maybe at its peak. Temptation was everywhere. I cheated, is the truth of it. A lot. Gemma deserved better. That's why I can't be mad that she never told me about Tim. I just can't be mad."

"But you are?"

Bodhi nodded slowly. "A little. Mostly at myself for being a loser."

Sailor was silent for a moment, studying him. He looked tired, his beautiful eyes had dark circles underneath, his whole body slumped. Sailor resisted the temptation to hug him or to smooth his dark curls away from his face. He was her boss after all, no matter how friendly and inclusive he was.

"What do you want, Bodhi? Out of life, I mean. You have every material thing a person could need; you have your son back in your life. What else is there?"

Bodhi met her gaze and smiled sadly. "I don't know, Sailor, is the honest truth. There's something missing, and I don't know what it is. I know I'm glad I found a new friend if that means anything."

Sailor grinned, flushing slightly. "Right back at you, boss."

"Gah, don't call me that. We're...collaborators in life."

Sailor laughed. "I like that." She glanced at her watch. "God, it's late. I'd better go."

Bodhi got up, and she followed him into the kitchen. He opened a small cabinet and took out a set of keys. "Here you go. You know how to drive right?"

Sailor nodded, taking the keys. Bodhi's fingers brushed hers, and a small thrill went through her. "Will you be okay driving home?"

She nodded. "Of course."

He walked her out to the car, and she couldn't help but gasp. It was a mint green Thunderbird, in spotless condition. Sailor shook her head. "I can't, Bodhi, this is too much."

"Sailor, this car was made for you. It's classy, classic and beautiful. Just like you."

There were tears in Sailor's eyes now, and she turned away from him. "Bodhi...you just met me, and already you've given me so much. I can't take it, I'm sorry."

"Then think of it as a loaner until you find one you like." He dumped the keys in her hand and steered her towards the car. His hands on her bare shoulders were soft, caressing and Sailor shivered. Nope, do not get a crush.

Bodhi would take no further argument. He kissed her cheek

and waved as she started down the long driveway to the road out.

As she drove home, Sailor's thoughts were in turmoil. Bodhi was kind, generous, funny and smart, but there was certainly a little control freak in him. Did she really want that in her life again? As she opened the door to her tiny apartment, she sighed. She didn't really have a choice, did she?

And besides, she was excited about the job, as well as spending time with Bodhi and Tim. She'd seen the pain in the little boy's eyes, reflected in his fathers who was unable to reach him. If she could help bring them together…

What? What's in it for you? She closed her eyes. I just want to feel useful. That I've made a difference, however small. Her mind flitted back to when Bodhi's hands were on her bare shoulders. The feelings that had flooded through her were unexpected and scary. Desire. Sailor tried to push the thoughts away as she stripped down and stepped into her shower, but she couldn't help but fantasize that Bodhi was in the shower with her, stroking her clit, kissing her mouth, his big arms around her, holding, protecting, loving. Her own hand snaked down and began to caress herself, masturbation had been a sin back in the commune, especially for the 'chosen bride', who was meant to save herself for Bartholomew. Which was why, at twenty-four, Sailor was still a virgin. A goddamned virgin, she thought angrily.

Sailor gritted her teeth for a second then returned to her fantasy. She would stroke Bodhi's cock until it was rigid and proud against his belly and then he would take her, impaling her on his cock, and fucking her hard until she was screaming his name.

Sailor's body was trembling all over as she stroked herself

into an orgasm, picturing Bodhi's beautiful face smiling down at her and whispering her name again and again.

A FEW MILES AWAY, Bodhi lay naked on his bed, staring up at the ceiling, his own mind whirling with desire, doubt, temptation. Sailor was his responsibility now, and he could not, would not take advantage of her, no matter how much he couldn't stop thinking about her smooth caramel skin, her dark eyes, that wave of soft hair almost to her waist. He could not compromise their working relationship; Sailor needed this job. It didn't matter how much he pictured her slowly stripping her clothes off, her large firm breasts, the curve of her waist, the deep hollow of her navel and that place between her legs that he so much wanted to taste.

No. There was a fragility to Sailor that he did not quite understand, and he would not be that guy anymore, the one who fucked around and didn't think of the other person. No. Sailor was his employee and, more than that, his friend. Whatever damage she had, he would help her heal from, as much as she would let him. He got the impression that she hated to be told what to do. Maybe he had pushed it a little far with the car, tonight. But he had been thinking about ways to thank her all evening, and when he thought of the Thunderbird, it fitted her aesthetic so well, it seemed natural.

Bodhi rolled over on his side and tried to fall asleep. Stop thinking about her...

Stop.

He didn't fall asleep until it was nearly dawn – and he didn't stop dreaming about Sailor.

SAILOR FELT her heart in her mouth as she drove excitedly up the driveway in the Thunderbird. First day of work. She and Bodhi were going to figure out a schedule for the next six months and then she could finally get started on her new career.

She pulled up to the door and got out. It was hot today and a fine sheen of sweat covered her as she left the air-conditioned car and knocked on the door.

A few seconds later, the door swung open and Bodhi grinned at her. "I forgot to give you a key, didn't I? Hey there, kiddo, first day." He kissed her cheek, and she blushed, grinning back. "Come have some coffee before we start."

He led her into the kitchen and Sailor felt her heart sink as she saw there was someone else there. A beautiful woman, no, strike that, a Goddess, stood chatting with Tim and sipping a mug of tea. She looked up and smiled at Sailor as they entered the room. She had long chestnut hair, straight down past her shoulders, and big friendly hazel eyes, almond-shaped. Sailor half-smiled back, unsure of what to feel. Jealous. That's what you are, admit it. She pushed the thought to the back of her mind.

Bodhi introduced them. "Sailor, this is Soleil, now that's not going to get confusing, is it?" He laughed. "Soleil is an old friend, my best friend, Claudio's sister."

Soleil put down her mug and came to give Sailor a hug. Her smile was genuine, her manner relaxed. "Ciao, Bella Sailor," she said in her broken English accent. "I've heard good things about you from these two. I'm very glad to meet you."

Sailor, warming to her, hugged her back. "And I, you. Hey, Tim," she said over Soleil's shoulder, and Tim waved his cereal spoon at her, his mouth full.

Soleil released her, but stood with her arm around Sailor's waist. "Now, before you start your job, let me warn you. Bodhi is an inveterate flirt. Don't let him run rings around you." She said it in a jokey tone, but Sailor knew she was telling her the truth and grinned at her boss. "I figured."

Soleil squeezed her. "Good girl. I'll get you some coffee."

"Thanks."

Bodhi waved her towards a seat then glared at his old friend in mock-anger. "Don't put her off me on her first day, Solly. Besides I don't flirt with everyone."

Solly snorted as she handed Sailor a mug of coffee. "You even flirt with me, and I'm practically your sister."

"Never worked though, did it?"

"I have taste. Besides, my heart belongs to another."

"Beyonce?"

"That's the one."

Sailor watched their playful banter, still a little envious of how easily they could joke with each other, but also seeing how platonic their relationship was. Tim was watching them too, even smiling at the teasing Soleil was giving his father.

Soleil left soon after, giving Sailor another hug. "Despite everything I tease him about, he's a good man," she said to Sailor, "I'm sure you'll love working for him. Sailor, do you know many people in L.A.? Bodhi said you've only been here for six months."

Sailor shook her head. "No-one. Unless you could call the clerk at the Seven Eleven a friend."

Soleil dug a pristine business card out from her purse. "Well, now you know someone new. Anytime you need some girl time, call me."

Sailor smiled shyly. "Thanks, I will."

BODHI GRINNED AT HER. "She's great, huh?"

Sailor nodded. "Lovely, really lovely."

women of Florence with abandonment. Soleil herself didn't

have time for relationships. At thirty-one, she was one of the most successful art dealers in the world and traveled constantly. Bodhi had harbored a crush on his friend's younger sister when he was younger, but Soleil, who had known about the attraction, had made it clear that it would never happen between them. Now they had cultivated a friendship, which was as important to Bodhi as his relationship with Claudio.

He grinned at Sailor. "So, I just have to take Tim to school then we can get started. Why don't you explore the house and grounds while we're gone? I'll be a half hour, tops."

"Okay."

If you want to continue reading this story, you can get your copy from your favorite vendor by searching for the title:

Rockstar Untamed
A Single Dad Virgin Romance

You can also find the e-book version by typing this link in your computer's browser:

https://www.hotandsteamyromance.com/products/rockstar-untamed-a-single-dad-a-virgin-romance

OTHER BOOKS BY THIS AUTHOR

Other Books By This Author

Saving Her Rescuer: A Billionaire & A Virgin Romance

I was just trying to get away from my crazy ex for the weekend when I ended up in a giant pileup on the highway up to Gore Mountain.

https://geni.us/SavingHerRescuer

∽

Sensual Sounds: A Rockstar Ménage

Lust. Lies. Double lives.

The rock and roll industry is full of people who are looking out for themselves and willing to do anything to rise to the top.

https://www.hotandsteamyromance.com/collections/frontpage/products/sensual-sounds-a-rockstar-menage

∽

On the Run: A Secret Baby Romance

Murder. Lies. Fraud. Just another day in the lives of billionaires and women on the run.

https://www.hotandsteamyromance.com/collections/frontpage/products/on-the-run-a-secret-baby-romance

The Dirty Doctor's Touch: A Billionaire Doctor Romance

I am a master. An elitist. I am at the top of my field, and I know what I am doing.

https://www.hotandsteamyromance.com/collections/frontpage/products/the-dirty-doctor-s-touch-a-billionaire-doctor-romance

The Hero She Needs: A Single Daddy Next Door Romance

He's the only man I've ever wanted…

https://www.hotandsteamyromance.com/collections/frontpage/products/the-hero-she-needs-a-single-daddy-next-door-romance

You can find all of my books here

Hot and Steamy Romance

https://www.hotandsteamyromance.com

ABOUT THE AUTHOR

Mrs. Love writes about smart, sexy women and the hot alpha billionaires who love them. She has found her own happily ever after with her dream husband and adorable 6 and 2 year old kids.
Currently, Michelle is hard at work on the next book in the series, and trying to stay off the Internet.
"Thank you for supporting an indie author. Anything you can do, whether it be writing a review, or even simply telling a fellow reader that you enjoyed this. Thanks

Facebook
facebook.com/HotAndSteamyRomance

COPYRIGHT

©Copyright 2020 by Michelle Love - All rights Reserved
In no way is it legal to reproduce, duplicate, or transmit any part of this document in either electronic means or in printed format. Recording of this publication is strictly prohibited and any storage of this document is not allowed unless with written permission from the publisher. All rights are reserved. Respective authors own all copyrights not held by the publisher.

www.ingramcontent.com/pod-product-compliance
Lightning Source LLC
LaVergne TN
LVHW021712060526
838200LV00050B/2619